# *Pharaoh Forever*

## PART I

## OBEDIENCE

## DEVIAN NIKEI

<u>*Other Nikei Novels by Devian Nikei*</u>

## Safety in Lovers

## Just in Case

## god face

# PART I

# OBEDIENCE

*Devian Nikei*

This book is a work of fiction. Names, characters, places and incidents are products of the author's imagination or are used fictitiously. Any resemblance to actual events or locales or persons, living or dead, is entirely coincidental.

## Copyright © 2016 Devian Nikei

ISBN: 0692723226
ISBN-13: 978-0692723227
BISAC: Suspense/Thriller/Historical Fiction

Interior design by Devian Nikei

Printed in the U.S.A.

A publication of Nikei Novels Publishing-Charlotte

To order copies and other merchandise or for more information, contact:

www.deviancebydevian.com
email: nikeinovels@deviancebydevian.com

# *Dedication*

I dedicate this book series; my most endearing and engrossing work, to my mother, Vivian- whose unsearchable, insatiable and unconditional love for me is the reason for everything that I am. Her advice and encouragement at my lowest times is the foundation of all my accomplishments. It is on her wings that I have known the height and depth and breadth of God's love.

*Devian Nikei*

*Shhhick... Shhhick*

This really ain't the best place to start.

*Barrrump... Shhhick.... Shhhick... Barrrump*

It wouldn't make a lot of sense if I started here.

*Shhhick.... Barrrump...*

This is how the story starts but it's not the beginning.

*Devian Nikei*

# THE BEGINNING
## (December 1972)

The beginning of a story is relative, I guess.

Stories are alive. They are dynamic; constantly changing and evolving as a result of the different actions or details which surround them. Stories can even change based on the teller.

Ask anyone what the beginning was and you will have as many different answers as people. Even if the beginning starts with "Let there be light"– a statement that most people accept definitively as *The Beginning,* then you would have to explain the void-

The void which covered the face of the deep... A void so immense that God created people and commanded them to replenish the earth... A command which begs the question: *what exactly are we **re-**plenishing?*

See what I mean? There is a story there, even back before *The Beginning*.

There are so many questions that I thought I would get the answers to here:

*- Why are there nine planets, but only one of them has life on it?*

*- How can there be so much poverty in a world that can afford so many wars?*

*- What is Charo really saying?*

*- Why did I have to die so young?*

And the list goes on and on.

But I didn't get any answers in this place- only the perpetual torture of not knowing the answers. That's all I got for my troubles.

### Shhhick... Barrrump... Shhhick

This story begins with my husband, Mason Rameses.

First off- no one around here knows him by that name. Three of the only four people to ever call him by it were the ones who gave it to him and me. But now that both of his parents are dead and I am too- the name is all but gone with us.

Everyone around here calls him **Pharaoh**... and they don't even know why. They think it's because he's a real Boss Nigger- the Black King Pin. They don't know that it's a play off his real name. Whatever the reasons they call him Pharaoh, it's more than a name or title to him. It's who he truly is: a god and ruler in his own mind.

Pharaoh is God's gift to women; a tall, slender, butter-pecan-tan man with a plan. Pharaoh stays super *fly*. He dresses sharper than a set of woodpecker lips. In his suede leisure suits and alligator skin boots, he is as fine to look at as his love is long... and the only thing longer than his love is his money. He's got beauty and money and sex for days, more than enough to spare... which he doesn't— spare, I mean.

Now Pharaoh is very generous and there's more than enough of him to go around. Because of the way he lavishes his love and money on his women, I never thought he would make me his *Main Squeeze*. I was surprised when he even *noticed* me and then actually *chose* me out from the crowd of foxes that flocked around his lap at the nightspot. I was just a waitress, only there to take his order, but what he ordered was me...*to go*, if you can dig it.

Now my story starts with an invitation from Pharaoh to breakfast after my shift. Pharaoh was so charming and ambitious back then. He was young; only twenty-five years old. He didn't yet know the ways of patience and temperance, seduction and manipulation- only passion and aggression, violence and satisfaction.

### Shhhick... Shhhick

I was even younger, only seventeen myself. I left home from

Georgia, on a bus headed out west to California. They told me it was live out here– a place to make dreams come true. Well if living in a shack and working in a dive is the dream, then call me Langston Hughes, baby.

In a city with no name, I myself have become nameless like my city. When I was alive, Pharaoh called me Belle because he said I reminded him of the singer, Patti Labelle. No one knew or even cared what my real name was, only what Pharaoh called me because he gave me life.

Before him, I was nothing. I was no one. That's what he led me to believe.

**Barrrump…. Shhhick… Barrrump**

... and believe it, I did.

What else was there to believe in?

I was the ninth of eleven children. The only thing my parents could afford to give me for graduation was the bus ticket to California. They figured it would be cheaper than living under their roof for another two years of community college.

I never had anything of my own before I met Pharaoh. I had to share my entire life. Even when I came to Cali, I lived in a one-bedroom, efficiency apartment with five other people; each of us scraping to get by. I slept on a pallet in the floor with food tucked into my bra and panties, just to make sure that I still had something to eat in the morning. Pharaoh changed all that for me. His money was enough to purchase my soul. His sex and his status were all just a bonus.

Mirage is different from me. She don't care about money. She's got more than enough of her own. Even right now, as we speak, Mirage is worth more money than most people make in a year. Money don't cut it for her. She's waiting for love. True love is the only cure for what ails her– but this is her story, not mine.

So let me begin at the beginning-

The beginning begins with Pharaoh digging a shallow grave for me in a forest somewhere east of Reno, Nevada.

**Shhhick....** *Pharaoh plunges his shovel into the dirt.*

Me– I'm not important to this story.

In fact, I'm so unimportant that no one even knows enough about me to tell my family that I am deceased. If they did know me, they would tell my mother that I have gone on to be with the Lord. But that would be a lie, 'cause I ain't seen the Lord nowhere around here. Still, in order for people to tell her that— first, they would have to know that I'm dead. But don't nobody know that neither 'cept for me and Pharaoh.

After four long, violent years together you would think he'd send me off better than this. I suppose this is the retirement plan for battered and abused wives. It's not so bad, I guess. At least I've got Jimmy here to keep me company.

**Barrrump...** *Clumps of earth hit the ground and scatter.*

When me and Pharaoh got married, it was all good... in the beginning of that story anyway. It was all flowers and candies, minks and chinchillas, diamonds and pearls. For every bloody nose or black eye he gave me, I had a treasury to show for it. I wish I knew then that I couldn't take any of it with me 'cause it's cold around here and I could sure use a fur.

**Shhhick, Shhhick.... Barrrump**

One day, Jimmy (Pharaoh's right hand man) came by to pick him up for a meeting. Pharaoh wasn't home and it was cold outside; so I told Jimmy he could wait for him inside the house.

I knew better.

Pharaoh don't like no men up in his crib when he ain't there, but come on... It wasn't nobody but Jimmy. I never understood why Pharaoh was so jealous. He didn't never have to worry about me stepping out. I loved him and no one else. He was the best— the only man I ever had. His long stroke kept my chocha so hot that it'd burn your fingers to the touch.

Jimmy hung around for a little while, but he didn't stay long. He said he'd look for Pharaoh down at the barbershop. I figured Jimmy found him 'cause I didn't see neither one of them again for two days...

When Pharaoh came through the door, late in the evening on the third day; I asked if he wanted something to eat. Instead of answering, he punched me in the face. He clutched my shirt in one fist and hit me mercilessly with the other. I felt my jaw break, right before the blow that knocked me unconscious.

I woke up in the trunk of his champagne-colored Cadillac Coupe Deville; crammed between shovels, oil canisters and only God knows what else. My mouth was covered with electrical tape. Pharaoh bound my hands and feet behind my back. I must've had a concussion because I threw up in my mouth a couple times during the trip. At one point, I thought I would drown on my own vomit before Pharaoh had the chance to kill me. I prayed and I prayed... and then I prayed some more to God in heaven that this was just another one of Pharaoh's scare tactics and not the real thing. But when we finally reached the destination, I was sure of two things– that there was no god except Pharaoh and that I had better beg *his* forgiveness if I wanted to live.

Unfortunately for me, I didn't get the chance... to beg, I mean. 'Cause I certainly would have. I would have done whatever he wanted me to do, as I had always done before. Sadly, the only thing he wants from me now is my life, so who am I to refuse him.

It won't mean nothing without him anyway.

### Pharaoh Forever

Now Pharaoh very rarely does any of his own dirty work; so this must be a special, intimate deed. To come all the way out here in the woods, so early on a cold, overcast winter morning. To murder me by his own hand is something that I could never have believed he would do. I watch him dig; his powerful arms making light work of the gravesite. His beige wool trench coat blows open in a gust of chilly wind. His hair, which usually lays in silky, shiny waves around his temples, is now a sweaty mess of tangled tresses. I beg his mercy with my pained eyes but I cannot compel his gaze. He disregards my muffled sobs and continues, undeterred, to dredge earth from the hole.

My eyes burn when he douses my body with gasoline. Pharaoh turns up each of the large red-tin containers, releasing a flood of slippery oil. As he soaks me from head to toe, I begin to panic and hyperventilate. Before I faint, he reaches down to pull the dog tags of his best friend Musah Franklin from around my neck. The clasp snaps from the force of the tug and the chain breaks free.

Musah's tags are the only set that he has and they have a very sentimental meaning to him. I don't know what it is though. Pharaoh has never talked to me about his military days or his experiences in Vietnam. As short-lived as his military career was, it has left scars on him. He's got shell shock and night terrors to prove it.

Pharaoh ensures that I am completely saturated with gasoline, then pulls out his embossed-silver lighter and a cigar. Once he establishes the orange glow at the end of his Cuban, he throws the lighter on me and I go up in flames like a pile of fall leaves.

Pharaoh doesn't even flinch, as he watches me burn. The flames tower high above him, casting long shadows over his body and he begins to sweat from the heat. His eyes are as hot with rage as my body is with fire. He's all-monster now; none of the man that I once loved is left. His eyes go completely black until there is no white left in them. The only light in his eyes is cast from the reflection of the flames.

I can't scream because I have no breath left in my body. I'm not conscious, but I can still feel the searing heat and the excruciating torture of my flesh roasting on the bones. Seconds later the pain is gone and replaced with euphoria. I know then that I'm a goner. The smoke fills my lungs, choking me out and putting me to sleep like a baby. The smoke holds me tightly in its embrace and gently rocks me into slumber... just like a little baby.

**Barrrump... Shhhick, Shhhick.... Barrrump.**

*Shhh... I sleep now*

# LOST ANGEL IN LAS VEGAS

## (December 1974)

Mirage is a lost angel in Las Vegas.

Men don't understand why she does what she does. She is gorgeous enough to have it made. Any man would love to wife her and give her the good life, but the good life is not what she chose. She chose instead, to become an exotic dancer; so lovely to behold that the owner– Myles, named her Mirage. With smooth, brown skin and large, dark doe eyes, her face is exotic and alluring. Her gorgeous visage is only eclipsed by her toned, voluptuous body. When she first walked into his strip joint, Myles said she was too beautiful to be real.

But she is real.

... and her real name is Cher Loussaint. She is the only child of two loving Creole parents. They moved to Las Vegas from New Orleans when Cher was only five years old. Her parents bought a diner-style restaurant just a few miles outside of the Vegas Strip on the edge of the desert. They made that little piece of dirt, their corner of heaven and were satisfied to dwell there together as a happy family.

Cher can still recall the nights she would wake in their trailer home and find her parents dancing together; just a simple slow drag in the moonlight. Her mother, Serafine, was dark-complexioned as mulatto women go; but she was beautiful with sharp, prominent cheekbones and wavy, raven-colored hair that reached down to her hips. Janvier, her father, tall and fair, doted on her mother as though she was the only woman on the earth.

Cher would watch them dance to a slow jazz 45 spinning on the record player. Cher's father would serenade her mother in his tenor voice, harmonizing with Doris Day-

"When I fall in love..." He smiles, as he sings. "...it will be forever."

Cher's father would twirl her mother around and around in smooth circles until her laughter woke Cher from her sleep. Then Cher would watch them dance, like in a fairy tale. Cher came to equate dancing with happiness because of the look on her mother's face when she swayed to the music.

When Cher's giddiness would overtake her, she'd run into the folds of her mother's skirt and throw her arms around her waist. They would laugh and laugh together. Then her father would put Cher's feet on top of his and she would dance between her parents. It was there, in the dance, that she felt their love. A love so full and so true that it was impossible for Cher to imagine any darkness or evil in the world. Still- Cher learned, all too early, that every big, bright light casts a long, dark shadow.

Her parents ran the diner for three successful years. Then one day, when she was eight, a band of robbers came in. Cher and her mother were out back by the trailer, hanging clothes on the line, when they heard the gun shots ring out from inside.

"Lock the door, Cher," Seraphine whispered, shoving her inside the trailer. "Hide ma petite!"

Those were her mother's last words to her.

The robbers raped and murdered her mother, before leaving with money and equipment from the diner. Cher always wondered why her mother didn't stay there with her. Why did she run to her father's aid? ... Especially knowing that she may not survive.

Cher could never understand, at that age anyway, how a love could be so strong between two people that you'd rather die than live without it– that you'd fight to the death, just as her mother had, trying to preserve it.

When the police found Cher in the trailer, hiding beneath her parents' bed, she was placed into the Child Welfare System. She didn't even know why she was there. She thought she was waiting for her mother and father to get out of the hospital and come for her. It was a few weeks of "when am I going home?" and "where are my parents?" before one of the other children explained to Cher what the term *orphan* meant. Cher punched the girl in the face and broke her nose. It took two other children and the night ward to get Cher off of her.

The only thing worse than growing up homeless in Vegas, is growing up in the welfare system. Las Vegas is a transient, tourist city. It's not a place where people come to start a family; but if they did, they would want babies. As gorgeous of a girl as she was, Cher was old as orphans go; so she was a difficult case for adoption.

Not that she much wanted to be adopted anyway; Cher was a terror for the first year. She had no other family or she would surely have run away. The other girls teased her for being pretty and having long hair. They hurled words at her, but none dared to lay a finger on her after the way she laid the *mollywop* on their companion.

Cher's beauty made her an outcast. She sat on her cot daily and tried to imagine what life outside of the facility would be like. They ate, drank, slept and went to school all within the confines of the same walls. Cher wondered what she could have done so wrong to deserve such a severe punishment.

When she wasn't dreaming by day, she was wrestling with demons at night. At nighttime, when darkness fell over the facility, Cher would hold her hands up in front of the tiny window in her corner of the dormitory. The bright neon lights from the strip club next door would flicker and flash between her fingers, casting long shadows across the floor. Cher would pull out the record that only she could hear and put it on the player in her mind.

"When I fall in love..."

She'd waltz the finger shadows around the floor, in rhythm with the strings, until the space became a ballroom and the shadows became the ghostly figures of her Prince Father and Princess Mother. Cher would even wiggle her pinky finger to conjure up a tiny image of herself, there in the dance with her parents.

"... It will be forever."

Then the snore of the girl in the bed next to her would shatter the illusion and bring Cher careening back to the reality that she was alone in the world. She would hide beneath her bed and spend the remainder of the night silently crying herself to sleep on the floor.

From the age of eleven to seventeen, Cher circulated through nine different foster homes. She never stayed in one home for very long. She would stay in some for a few weeks, a few months, or on an occasion or two, even a year or better.

The length of her stay depended on the determination of the foster parents. Some cared for Cher and wanted desperately to keep her. But once they learned that the place in a child's heart that is usually cold-wired for love had blown out in Cher, they sat her out on the curb like a defective stove oven for the garbage man to pick up.

Cher was never the right fit for the families that would take her in. Usually, she was out before she even had time to unpack. She would forget the families by the time she left. Even now, when she thinks back to those years, only one of them comes to mind– her first foster home, The Jenkinses. They kept Cher for two whole years- the longest of any *family*.

Cher came into the home of Reverend and Mrs. Shelton Lamar Jenkins, when she was eleven years old. "They is a good, *Christian* family. God just never saw fit to bless them with children of their own." The social worker advised Cher.

The Reverend shepherded a sizeable congregation in Henderson. They weren't rich by any measure, but they lived relatively comfortable by colored standards. All Cher needed to do was be a good girl and she could find happiness in their home. Cher found a lot of things in their home- mostly secrets, but happiness was not one of them.

The Reverend and Mrs. were tall, lanky creatures and both wore horn-rimmed glasses. They were as black as cast-iron. Mrs. Jenkins was uninviting, tight-lipped and strict. She treated Cher like a modern-day Cinderella, instilling that her only value was domestic. Mrs. Jenkins would smack the back of Cher's hand with a ruler for everything from dropping clothes she brought in from the line to slouching in her chair at the dinner table. Cher began to think that the ruler was as permanent an appendage as Mrs. Jenkins's right hand itself.

Reverend Jenkins, however, was quite different when out of the watchful eye of the Mrs. He doted on Cher, bringing her tiny gifts and trinkets, candies and hair bows. The Reverend was always kind and polite to her, but there was something about him that Cher didn't like.

It was the way he licked his lips while holding out a Sugar Daddy or Bit-O-Honey for her to take from his hand. It was the way that he would grab her hand when she reached for it. The Reverend would hold Cher's hands, and dance her around, spinning her in circles. But the love was not there, in the dance, as it had been with her parents.

When the Mrs. went to visit the sick and the shut in, Reverend Jenkins would bring Cher down into the basement of the house and sit her on his lap for story time.

Now, Cher was *way* too old for sitting on laps and listening to stories, but the Reverend insisted it was essential for family bonding. Cher couldn't explain the overwhelming wrongness that welled up in her spirit when the Reverend rubbed his fingers over her private parts. Cher had not yet found the name for it- a term that could best describe it. But as the months passed in that house and the touching turned into prodding, and the prodding into penetration, the feeling finally found its identity in one word-

## *Shame*

It was during the second year that Cher stopped bleeding. When her menstrual started, the Mrs. was careful to teach Cher about her body. She showed her how to take care of herself, so she wouldn't catch the *Nasty Girl's Disease*. Cher didn't know who else to turn to when the bleeding stopped. She didn't know what it could mean. But Mrs. Jenkins knew and wouldn't answer any of her questions.

Instead, she took Cher to see the *doctor*; another tall, impossibly Black creature wearing a sweat-stained undershirt and soiled denim overalls. He straightened a wire clothes hanger and told Cher to lay down on a bed sheet that covered his kitchen table. The roaches scattered to give them room to conduct the *procedure*. A dim fluorescent bulb overhead gave off just enough light to illuminate the room, as it buzzed and flickered its last.

On their way to the *clinic,* the Mrs. finally told Cher that she must have swallowed some watermelon seeds that were growing on the inside of her stomach. "If the doctor doesn't get them out right away, you will die," Mrs. Jenkins stated evenly with steady, unblinking eyes.

Cher shrieked in pain while the Mrs. sat comfortably on a dilapidated sofa in the living room. She had never experienced an agony so excruciating. Cher figured that Mrs. Jenkins must have been right about those melons; the dark, bloody balls that the doctor pulled from inside of her. They must have been a very bad thing because she felt like she was going to die when they were removed. Cher was thankful to the Mrs. for taking her to get treatment. Cher thought Mrs. Jenkins might just care for her after all–

Until the next day, when she dropped Cher back off at the orphanage. The Mrs. told the social workers that Cher was incorrigible and could no longer be tolerated in their home. Cher wasn't hurt. She was accustomed to rejection by then; but what did hurt- was her stomach. An increasingly bitter pain began to spread through her pelvis and thighs. Cher thought she was okay because the bleeding had started again. Cher believed that bleeding was a good thing which happens naturally in a young woman's body. Cher continued to believe that until she passed out in Home Economics, two days later.

Cher was hospitalized for a week. The doctors spoke to the social workers describing things in words that Cher didn't understand. After that, Cher was placed into other homes, but she was always visited often and monitored closely. She would never again have to worry about any of those stomach melons.

When Cher was released from the custody of the system, she was advised that her parents had endowed her with a trust fund in the amount of twenty thousand dollars. The money had been placed in an account to accrue interest until her eighteenth birthday. Cher didn't even care about the money. It will be many years and several thousands of dollars later before she ever even touches that money.

Even at eighteen, Cher realized that money couldn't fix what was broken in her. She took the stipend that she saved over her nine years in the system, a mere $496, and walked out of the Children's Home with nothing but the clothes on her back. She strode out of the front door, down the walkway, through the gate, up the sidewalk, across the parking lot and into The Thoroughbred Lounge.

# TROUBLE MAN

"I love to love you, baby…"

Mirage crawls out on to the stage and rolls over on her back, letting the melody wash over her in waves.

"I love to love you, baby…"

Mirage loves this song. Myles won't let none of the other girls dance to it. This is *her* song. Hell- this is *her* spot. Mirage runs everything around here because she keeps the house full. She is the main attraction, much to the chagrin of the other dancers.

Mirage loves Donna Summer. Mirage wants to **be** Donna Summer and dance around like she is on a cloud all day. Mirage braided her long, brown hair into painful cornrows and wore them for three days- just for tonight… All so she could look like Donna Summer with flowing hair cascading in soft, silky waves down her back.

For Mirage, Saturday nights are no huge occasion. She brings in at least five hundred dollars every week, without even trying. Mirage doesn't have to try. She doesn't even have to dance if she doesn't want to.

One night, about six months ago, Mirage came out on stage fully dressed in a coral-colored, sleeveless satin romper. She looked like she was dressed for watching T.V. on her sofa. She pulled a barstool out and sat it in the middle of the stage, then went back and told the deejay not to spin any records at all. When Mirage returned, she had a glass of milk in one hand and a box of Barnum's Animal Crackers in the other. Mirage sat on stage in silence, drinking milk and eating cookies for nine minutes, as though she was at home in her own kitchen. The audience was silent at first; completely confused by her act. A few hecklers began to whistle and yell catcalls, but Mirage didn't even acknowledge them with a glance.

Myles was sure that she had flipped her wig. He was dreading the fact that he was gone have to fire her… until the first few dollar bills fell on the stage. Men began to throw tens, and then twenties on the stage and cheer for her as she sipped the last of the milk, letting the final drops drip down on her tongue.

Myles couldn't believe it and neither could the other girls in the back. Mirage did a courteous bow, collected her earnings and stuffed over a hundred dollars into her bra before exiting the stage, dragging the barstool behind her. The other dancers would surely have strangled her backstage, if they didn't fear her-

*But they do fear her...*

Everybody, including Myles, does. Something about that damn Mirage ain't wrapped too tight. They can't put their finger on it. She looks cool to the naked eye, but they all know she's bugged out.

On another night, a couple years ago, she was walking to the bar to get a ginger ale and a customer grabbed her arm. Mirage stopped and gave him a death stare. Obviously, no one told him that Mirage doesn't give lap dances. He waved a fifty-dollar bill in front of her. Mirage yanked her wrist back, but before she could finish her trip to the bar, the man grabbed her around the waist. Faster than you can say "Mirage", she broke his beer bottle on the table and held the jagged edge against his throat. Security came to escort the customer out of the club before Mirage could make him a eunuch. Even still, the incident made everyone question her sanity.

"I... love to love you, baby..."

Mirage has been laying on the stage for about five minutes now. She's just enjoying the song. Donna Summer's sultry, wispy voice transports her to a state of relaxation. Mirage lifts her legs and makes circular motions with her ankles.

Mirage came prepared to dance tonight. She wore her new outfit; a sheer body stocking with shiny, silver sequins covering her private areas. She wasn't going to strip. She just wanted to dance. Mirage was going to let the pulsing, glittery lights of the disco ball flash over her and then the sequins, reflecting the glare, would transform her into a celestial body. Mirage imagined herself twinkling like a star while she spun around the pole.

*This is why she dances*

It is for her own pleasure and not for a living. She could care less about those jive turkeys out in the audience. She thinks it's laughable that they are even willing to pay to see her dance. She would still dance, even if she wasn't paid to. You could catch Mirage every day of the week, bopping along, shuffling her feet and shaking her hips at any one of the discotheques along the Vegas strip.

Dance courses through her veins like blood. She isn't even that good at it, as far as dancers go. She has no training, but who needs that when you have the passion for it that Mirage does. And where passion and potential fail her, beauty fills in all the gaps. Mirage hates crowds and strange men touching on her. So other than the added bonus of getting paid, Mirage gets to dance at the Thoroughbred Lounge, uninhibited and undisturbed, for nothing more than her own entertainment.

Mirage decides after another few minutes that despite all the effort she put into her hair and outfit, she is not going to dance. She rolls over on to her stomach and presses herself up into a middle split. The men in the gallery begin to howl. By her calculation, there is already about ninety dollars on the stage, which was placed there while she was still just laying down. That is more than enough money for her to make cash out and take in a late movie, or maybe some early breakfast and whatever other whims she may have. Mirage brings her legs together and bends them at the knees. She crosses one ankle over the other and pulls herself to her feet. She struts around the pole twice. The money on the stage has doubled already. Mirage leans away, supported only by her left arm. She death drops on to the stage, spins on her back and then pops back up to her feet- all in one swooping motion while still holding the pole. The men are on their feet cheering when Mirage begins to walk off the stage. She hasn't even done anything that spectacular and she knows it, but she doesn't care. She is bored and tonight is like so many before.

She has been waiting for something.

*Something- but what?*

She doesn't know what it is- but she knows that she will know it when she sees it. As she turns to exit behind the curtain, she sees-

**Him**

*Has he been there all along?*

She stops at the edge of the curtain. She can't see out into the gallery very well. The bright lights blind her. Cher shields her eyes with her hand and can faintly make him out at the back of the club. He sits in the reserved section behind rows of colorful, stringed beads.

His limbs are long. Cher can tell even in a seated position that he is very tall. He is slender, but something about the way he sits shows his strength and authority. He is poised, almost regal, in a cream, three-piece suit with wide disco lapels. His multi-colored, paisley shirt is unbuttoned, revealing light chest hair and a heavy gold-pyramid medallion hanging around his neck. His shiny, wavy hair is combed back away from his face, falling just below his collar. He has a ring on every finger of his right hand, but it's not his affluent attire that has Mirage's attention. It's his hauteur- his hubris. He is **The Man** and she can tell it from over twenty yards away.

*Can he see me?* She wonders... but of course he can.

Pharaoh sees everything.

Cher comes out to the end of the platform. The men are at the edge of the stage making such a fuss about her coming back. The commotion gets Pharaoh's attention. He is always alert to changes in his atmosphere; especially when he is conducting business. Any subtle disturbance can signal serious consequences, if not heeded. His eyes connect with hers. Once Pharaoh is sure that Mirage is the source of the uproar, his focus returns to the two gentlemen on his right.

The two men with him have also turned to check out the vixen onstage, but unlike Pharaoh they are unable to detach from the vision they have just beheld. Pharaoh is visibly irritated by their lack of professionalism. Pharaoh never connects the two in his mind. Business is on one end of the spectrum with pleasure tucked way down at the other end.

As a matter of fact, after I (his beloved Belle) expired, Pharaoh changed his priorities. Women have become a momentary amusement for him; just the satiation of a carnal instinct. He decided that love was too expensive for him, and being as frugal as he is sexy, settled on occasional recreational sex with foxes instead of steady relationships. A decision that Pharaoh has found is better for his business, the only woman he will every truly love and respect. He trusts in his business because she has never double-crossed him. She does what he tells her to do and she is loyal to him. For Pharaoh, making money is better than sex– because it lasts longer. His business will always be number one.

Two snaps of his fingers bring the attention of the other men back to the table. Mirage wilts inside to see that the object of her affection is not as taken with her as the whole rest of the club. Attempting to recapture his focus, she drops down letting her bottom touch the back of her heels. She spreads her knees apart and whips her hair down between her legs; a feat both of strength and balance. The crowd cheers. The patrons are on their feet, but Pharaoh talks on intently. She sits back and spreads her legs into a wide V. One turkey comes to the edge of the stage and places his face in the space between her bottom and the edge. Ordinarily, Mirage would be disgusted, but she has no time for that now. She is on a mission to get the attention of the tall, fair stranger at the back of the club. Mirage rolls over backwards, sliding into a split. There is so much money on the stage that she has to dance on top of it. Mirage rolls in the bills, lifting them above her head and letting them fall over her buxom breasts. Pharaoh hasn't looked at her once, but the other men with him have. Mirage doesn't want their eyes. She wants only his.

*Look at me*

*Watch me;* she beckons to him with her spirit. Mirage begins to seduce herself with the thought of seducing him. She concentrates her efforts on him. She tries to conjure an invisible energy that will draw his eyes to her body. This is her best performance ever because it's just for him. Mirage is finally dancing for someone other than herself and the audience is getting off on his account.

All of her sorcery could not enchant him and before the song ends, the noise from the audience coupled with the stunner on stage provide too much distraction from Pharaoh's business meeting. He stands up from the table and closes the door. Mirage, feeling like an abandoned orphan, marches angrily offstage to an ovation of cheers and applause from the gallery.

**\*\*\*\***

The next night when Mirage took the stage, she half-expected that the picturesque stranger would be there; maybe in a less professional capacity. She came out to the edge of the platform and scanned the room. When she didn't see him anywhere, she walked offstage to a mix of awes and boos. She sat in the dressing area for a few minutes, dejected and depressed, but then thought the better of it.

*I don't even know him*

*Why should I be upset?*

Mirage is so despondent at the absence of her paramour that she undresses and throws on some fitted, patch-denim bell-bottoms. She slips her feet into a pair of yellow, open-toe platform sandals and then ties the collar of a red satin, bell-sleeved blouse into a bow at her neck. She labors to pull her mass of wavy hair into an elastic band. Mirage twists strands of hair and sticks pins in to secure her up-do. Turning side to side, Mirage adjusts the twists until she is satisfied with her reflection. The other half-naked stellas walk back and forth past her dressing table, pissed that she can afford to take the night off. They can't stand her. They think that she thinks she is better than them. The truth is that Mirage doesn't care enough about any one of them to even compare herself. As far as she is concerned, none of them even exist in her world.

Mirage blows herself a kiss to the mirror before striding out the door. When she steps on to the sidewalk, a brisk night breeze wraps her in its icy embrace. She throws her gray-and-white, rabbit fur coat across her shoulders. For the first time in a long time, she glances over at the Children's Home. Mirage cannot believe that three years later, she is still next door to a place that she vowed she would never see again after her release. It's strange how the world can be such a big and small place, all at the same time. Being confined to an institution for the better part of her life has made her long for freedom; the liberty that only music can give. The rhythm of a drum, like a heartbeat, gives life to her existence. She thought that dance would free her, but as she looks through the barbed wire fence that surrounds the grounds, she realizes that she has traded one prison for another.

*What are you waiting for?*

*Why don't you just leave?*

*And go where?*

*Go anywhere... or everywhere, but here*

Mirage begins to move her meditation along the sidewalk. She drifts along like an autumn leave driven by the wind. She stares at her feet as one drops down in front of the other.

*That's the spirit...*

*Follow each one until they take you where you want to go.*

*But where do you want to go?*

*I don't know.*

*Am I supposed to?*

Mirage stops in front of the movie theater. The marquee reads "Foxy Brown" on one side and "Uptown Saturday Night" on the other. She continues on. She has seen both films a couple times each. Besides, the strong Black females depicted on the screen would make her feel even more pathetic than she already does.

*What are you waiting for?*

She spins the idea around like a coin, but can't make heads or tails of it. She turns the corner and begins the walk to her deluxe apartment near Paradise Park. As she treks along, headlights from an oncoming car illuminate the street before her. Mirage figures that the driver will just speed by until she hears the tires decelerating. The car slows to a crawl, lurching along beside her. She doesn't even dignify the driver with a glance. Mirage assumes that he takes her for a Lady of the Night, so she quickens her steps. The champagne colored, cream-top Cadillac Coupe Deville continues to creep along beside her as she rounds the second corner.

"Look here turkey," she hisses forcefully. "I don't know what kind of trip you think this is, but-"

The car stops

It's **him-**

The sexy stranger from the lounge is sitting behind the wheel. Mirage chokes so hard on her words that she wants to cough them up. She closes her lips tightly instead.

"Do you need a ride?" He asserts lowly, with so much authority that she can't refuse him. It isn't a question, but rather a command disguised as an invitation.

"I don't feel comfortable getting into the car with a stranger." Cher replies cautiously.

"You are walking alone in the middle of the night in Las Vegas. I'm sure there's more to be afraid of out there than there is in here." He throws his arm behind the headrest and leans across the passenger seat. "I won't bite you Little Red Riding Hood." He smiles, displaying his prominent canine teeth. His dark eyes twinkle in the glowing neon lights of a nearby diner.

Mirage takes her time and studies him. He is dressed, more casual than before, in a navy turtleneck under a funky dashiki with brown leather pants. He edited himself down from the handful of jewelry he wore last night to one heavy, gold pinky ring and another slender band on his thumb. Cher can't help but think that he looks absolutely gorgeous. He's more attractive and younger than he appeared at the nightspot. He has Mirage so stunned that she doesn't realize how long she's been standing at his door.

"Foxy Mama, you can climb in and give those feet a break, if you want." Again, not a question, but a cleverly cloaked directive.

"Are you going to take me straight home?"

He crosses his heart and holds up his right hand. "Straight home... I promise."

Mirage opens the door and slinks carefully into the cool, soft red-leather passenger seat.

"Are you comfortable?" he asks sincerely; relieved that she has joined him. He stares into her eyes and Mirage instantly feels insecure– not out of fear, but because of her ravenous desire for him. He is still waiting patiently for her answer, so she nods slowly.

"Good." He offers his hand to her. "My name is Pharaoh."

She places her hand in his and he kisses it before covering it with his other hand. Mirage's knees tingle, a feeling she hasn't experienced in a *very* long time.

"Now that I'm not the stranger anymore..." He smiles again. Mirage looks away to keep him from seeing her blush. "What's your name?"

"Mirage," she whispers, staring out of the window.

"No-" Pharaoh cuts her short with a direct tone. He places a soft fingertip under her chin and turns her face to his. "I asked your name."

"My name is Cher," she answers sheepishly. The name seems so foreign to her. She hasn't said it for many years.

"A beautiful name for a beautiful woman."

He sits back in his seat. His eyes drift over her face. His expression is not one of lust– it's too distinguished for that. Pharaoh observes Cher like a king appraising his territory, surveying his conquered lands.

"My apartment is not that far away." Cher breaks the thick, suffocating silence.

"Solid," Pharaoh responds casually. He shifts the car into gear and slowly pulls away from the curb.

Pharaoh drives along quietly. As Cher traces his features, she feels compelled to touch him– to see if he is real. His pale, creamy skin is almost flawless, save a dark mole on his right cheek. Cher watches him carefully, as he adjusts his grip on the large steering wheel. His gold, chain-linked bracelets slide down on his forearm. His shapely lips purse beneath a full, neat moustache. She finally figures it out, but only after riffling through years and years of buried memories.

*That's it... That's what it is*

*Her father*

Pharaoh reminds Cher of her father. Of course, this man is very different; flashier and (dare she say) more handsome than Janvier Loussaint, but the same tall, slender frame and sun-kissed complexion. That is Cher's attraction. It has been so long since she even entertained the thought of her father. She begins to swoon for Pharaoh immediately. She sits beside him while they speed along and for the first time in a long time Cher feels...

## *Safe*

"Wait a minute," she blurts abruptly. "Where are we going?"

"I'm taking you home," he replies simply, not taking his eyes off of the highway.

"I never told you where I live and this is not the way."

"Yes, it is... This is definitely the way home," he offers with finality.

Cher begins to catch on to Pharaoh's talk game. "Tell it to me straight, sucker!" She sasses. "Where are you taking me?"

"To Los Angeles."

Cher's mouth drops open at the prospect. "Pull over and let me out right now. I didn't sign up for that."

Pharaoh pulls the car over on the shoulder of the road and turns off the engine. Cher's eyes scan the scene. The highway is completely deserted– no cars coming from either direction. Only stars, dirt, mountains and darkness surround them. Cher begins to perceive the predicament into which she has placed herself.

"You really don't want to come with me?" Pharaoh asks, completely surprised and confused. "You don't want me to take you home?"

"I don't know what kind of jive you running, but you can just take me right back to **my** apartment." Cher crosses her arms over her chest and produces a determined pout.

"But is that what you really want?" Pharaoh asks mildly with his eyes locked in on hers. She feels an invisible force. His energy, his spirit is so consuming that it threatens to suck her soul right out of her body. Cher, awestruck by him, fails to answer in the time allotted. "Well, I'm not going back to Vegas. My business there is done. My men have gone on ahead to L.A. and they will expect me there in a few hours."

"If everyone left already, then why did you stay behind?"

"I had one more asset that I wanted to acquire– just for myself." Pharaoh folds his hands on top of his thigh.

"I don't know what type of chick you think I am, but it ain't pay-for-play over here." Cher is visibly offended, but Pharaoh is far more insulted.

"Do I look like the type of brother who needs to buy a stella off the street?"

Pharaoh begins to rap to Cher; you know, real smooth on the language, but intense with his tone. "You really don't know who I am, do you?" He issues threateningly with furrowed brows. "I am **Pharaoh**." He pats his chest.

"That's more than a name. That is my title. I can have any fox I want." He wags his long pointer finger. "... and believe you me- I won't have to buy her. I don't take no stray ass pussy to my crib. They got motel rooms for that, you dig. Nothing but the finest for me, Mama... and I think you're it. As far as I can see, you are Grade A premium *filet mignon*, in my book, baby. I want you for myself because that club doesn't deserve you. A diamond as ice cold as you can only belong on my chain." Pharaoh shrugs his shoulders and lets his hands come back to rest in his lap.

Just when Cher begins to consider his invitation, Pharaoh turns on her.

"But... maybe I'm wrong. Maybe your mind ain't as grown as

your body. If you can't see rolling with a Boss Niggah like me, then you can just beat the bricks back down the road." He reaches across her body and pushes the passenger door open.

This is true Pharaoh style. Cher is stuck right between feeling seduced and insulted. She's not even sure which she's more upset about– what he said to her or being rejected by him. This rejection stings like nothing Cher has felt in a long time. Cher left rejection at the Children's Home and has not since been acquainted with it in her adult life. She wouldn't have even known what to call it, if it had not been for overhearing other females talk about it. This *rejection* is something that she is sure she never wants to experience again. It ignites a jealousy like fire in her bones.

*What are you waiting for?*

She issues the challenge to herself and (in answering herself) reaches out to grab the handle of the car door. She exhales long, then pulls the door closed and sits back against the seat.

"Are you sure?" Pharaoh asks with reservation. He sits, stately and magnificent, in the driver's seat like it is a throne. Pharaoh decimates Cher to a child, a mere worshipper before him. She loves it though, to feel so small in his divine presence. She is used to running the show; but is happy to concede to him, if it means satisfying her yearnings.

"Yeah, Boss. It's yo' thang." She pulls her fur from around her shoulders and places it in her lap.

"Right on," he says, leaning across to her door and securing the lock. When he sits back, he allows his lips to touch hers. His kiss is strong, but his lips are soft. Cher melts beneath the heat of them. She sinks down into the seat, his passion weighing heavy on her. Cher's lips are thick and supple. Pharaoh feels the burn in his loins, as he sucks on them. Pharaoh pauses to gaze into her eyes. Cher looks exhilarated and overwhelmed like a kid on an amusement ride. He sits back in his seat and grips the steering wheel so tightly that his knuckles whiten.

"Alright," Pharaoh growls lowly. His tone is reserved and resigned, as he quells his arousal. The ride back to L.A., usually a short trip, will be a very long one tonight. Despite all of Pharaoh's obstinate frigidity, he can be quite a passionate man. He feels so deeply, perhaps too deeply for a man with as many demons as he has.

"Let's burn the road up," he says with his eyes forward. He revs the engine, kicking up a huge cloud of dust and rocks before pulling his Cadillac back on to the highway.

# CALIFORNIA DREAMING

Cher doesn't know how to take this Pharaoh character.

She can't quite get a read on him. She doesn't even know him. The realization hits her like the first rays of dawn piercing the darkness. What seemed like a fairy tale last night is an eerie reality in the morning light. Cher half-expected to wake up in her own bed with a hangover. But when she woke between Pharaoh's navy satin sheets underneath a beaded canopy, she realized that she was not in Vegas anymore.

Pharaoh lives in quiet luxury on the north side of Los Angeles. Early in the morning, while it was still dark outside; they pulled up in front of a high-rise apartment building. The building with its pointed peak and sharp angles, more dark glass than anything else, looked like a huge black prism. Astonishment covered Cher's face when it came into view. She had never seen people live in anything like it before. One of Pharaoh's men, a short, brawny light-skinned brother that he referred to as Blaze, took the car keys from him. Once Pharaoh helped Cher out of the Cadillac, Blaze drove out of sight.

Pharaoh lives in the penthouse, high above the city on the fourteenth floor. He resides alone on that floor with no one to watch him come or go from his apartment. Pharaoh inserts a key in the elevator board to reach his level. Once inside his place, Pharaoh shows Cher around.

His pad is so disco, with green shag carpet and African artifacts everywhere. He takes Cher to his bedroom on the bottom level, so she can shower and sleep. Pharaoh showered in a separate bathroom, up the spiral staircase, on the second level of the apartment, and then slept up there. At least that's what Cher suspects happened. She wasn't really even sure if he slept at all. He was awake long before her.

When she enters the living room wearing only his San

Francisco 49ers jersey, Pharaoh is already ironing his white Egyptian linen leisure shirt. Pharaoh looks just as majestic, but more domestic in his own abode. He stands well-postured, in his gray undershirt and navy wide legged trousers. Pharaoh, in true pimp form, has his hair tied up in a red bandana.

"Good morning, Cher." He turns off the iron and wraps up the cord. "I was waiting for you to get up so we could have breakfast together."

Pharaoh is polite. He pulls a yellow vinyl chair away from the circular wood table for her and then steps into the kitchen. Pharaoh retrieves two plates covered with aluminum foil from the oven. He places them on the stovetop and uncovers them before turning the oven's low setting to off. Pharaoh, careful not to burn his soft, manicured hands, grabs the plates with a dish towel and takes them to the table. Cher studies him while he pours two glasses of milk and brings napkins from the kitchen. His arms and shoulders are lean, but powerful. Cher bites down on her lip, as she watches him work.

Likewise, Pharaoh is checking Cher out too. He finds her more gorgeous and real today than last night. He watches his reflection in her dark, doe eyes like shimmering black pools. He spent the entire trip back to L.A. wondering if bringing her back was a mistake. Pharaoh has lived here alone for years now. Never has a woman stepped foot into this place. Pharaoh picks out his women like he picks out his clothes and cars. With Pharaoh, it's not about color or fashion– whatever he chooses just has to fit. His woman has to compliment his lifestyle and fulfill his purpose for her.

Pharaoh watches Cher place a forkful of scrambled eggs into her mouth. She chews, not too dainty but not too ghetto either.

He approves of her. *Good choice,* he thinks to himself while sizing her up. Cher is so beautiful to him without any make-up and her hair in disarray. The strands that have come loose from her up do, wind their way down past her shoulder blades.

"It's not cold, is it?" he asks without taking a bite of his own food.

"No, it's just fine," Cher answers nervously.

"Something is wrong," Pharaoh says with serious urgency. "I can tell that you're not comfortable."

"Well," Cher starts hesitantly. "It's just that I don't have any clothes to wear."

Pharaoh unknits his brows and a coy smile spreads slowly across his face. When he smiles, Cher is instantly amazed by him. He transforms from a staunch potentate into a tender angel.

"I should have known that a woman like you could be disquieted by such a trivial matter as her threads." Pharaoh winks at her. "I think you look smoking just like this."

He frames her face with his fingers, letting his eyes drift down to her smooth, firm thighs.

"That ain't no thang, Mama." Pharaoh walks over and pulls out a couple of catalogues from the magazine rack beside his sofa. "Pick out whatever you want and I'll have it brought here for you, within the hour."

Pharaoh retrieves a thick roll of money from his pocket. "Take this." He slides three fifty dollar bills out of his gold money clip. "I'll leave my main man, Musah, here. He can take you out shopping on Rodeo Drive whenever you are ready." Pharaoh presses the money into her hand. "And if that's not enough... This is yours." Pharaoh gives her a credit card.

"Ummm–" Cher stammers. She is unsure of what to say. She

stares wide-eyed at the money in one hand and the credit card in the other. "Okay... Thank you."

"I've got business meetings all morning," he says casually, sliding his arms into his shirt. "After the trip to Vegas, my associates and I have a lot of prospects to discuss." Pharaoh walks into his bedroom. He emerges minutes later, with his hair perfectly groomed, wearing a silver Cartier wristwatch and a huge silver ring on his pointer finger. He buttons his shirt quickly.

"You missed one." Cher rises from the table.

"Missed one what?"

"A button hole." She comes over to him, both nervous and anxious to touch him. She unbuttons his shirt at the missed hole and then continues to button down to his waist.

"There... Perfect." She smiles.

"It sure is," Pharaoh breathes, looking into her eyes. He leans to kiss her. Cher closes her eyes and presses up on her toes. She wants to see if the magic from last night is still there. She is surprised when Pharaoh's lips land on her cheek.

"I'll see you a little later on, Mama. I want to take you out to dinner tonight, if that's alright?" He requests sheepishly, like a school boy asking a young girl out on a date.

Cher nods her head. Pharaoh smiles, like a sigh of relief, as if he expected her to refuse. That is his charm, the way he makes you feel important– the way he lets you choose him, as if you had any other choice. He starts for the door, but then stops abruptly.

"Hey Cher." A look of concern covers his face. "I forgot to tell you a few things."

He waits for her full attention.

"This is the key to my apartment." Pharaoh takes the long, silver chain, which holds the key, from around his neck and places it around hers. "You can't get up here without it. It's the *only* one- not even the building manager has another one, so **don't** lose it."

Cher nods attentively, careful to hang on every word. "Also, I don't allow anyone in my apartment when I am not here- *especially* not men. **Absolutely** no men in my apartment. You are the only person welcome in my crib without my express permission. Understand?"

Cher nods slowly. Pharaoh's eyes darken when he issues the command. If his tone was not indication enough of how serious he was; then his eyes, fierce and fervent, sealed the deal. Cher realizes in that moment that Pharaoh is quite possibly a very dangerous man.

"I'll be back around three, so I need you here to let me in." His eyes soften again. "I'll buzz you on the intercom, okay?"

"Alright," Cher peeps quietly, not sure if she can ask questions. She figures the less she knows at this point, may be the better. Pharaoh disappears behind the door.

*What kind of man leaves a strange woman alone in his apartment?*

Cher wanders through the rooms downstairs. On the first floor is his bedroom and the dining room which opens to the kitchen across from the living room. Cher thinks that Pharaoh's crib is so fab. He has a 30-inch, color television in his living room. Two cream-colored velour Tulip armchairs sit at each end of the brown, suede-leather sofa. All of the furniture is covered with large decorative throw pillows. A fully-stocked bar sits at the rear of the living room. Cher decides to take a look around the top floor. She climbs the spiral staircase ascending through the hole in the ceiling-floor. It is dark on the second level. The tinted glass ceiling keeps out more light than one would expect. There are two doors on that level, but both are locked. Cher can only imagine what lay behind them. The mystery prompts her to pose a question to herself-

*Just what is Pharaoh's business?*

Cher gasps at the question, realizing how unsafe it is for her not to know. Cher is angered by her ignorance, but she determines to push the flood of alarming images from her mind as she descends back down the stairs. Cher walks over to the floor-to-ceiling window wall on the west side of Pharaoh's apartment. The sun hasn't made its way over to this side of the building yet, but she can imagine how the sun descending into the ocean will look while lying on his sofa. In this castle tower, Cher feels like a queen. She looks afar off and can see the waves cresting and crashing on the beach. At the corner of her view, in the distance, she can see the sign which used to read **HOLLYWOOD,** but now only says **HULLYWO D**. All the same, the missing and damaged letters don't take away the wonder of what the sign represents.

Cher sighs deeply, feeling overwhelmed by the beauty of the scenery. She has missed so much of the world living in the Las Vegas slums. The view of the populated countryside bathing in golden light does the trick and soon her mind is free of all the panic she felt moments earlier. Cher picks up the catalogues from the dining room table and drops down into the comfort of the fluffy sofa cushions.

She flips through the pages of Macy's and Sak's Fifth Avenue advertisements. All of it is just a little too square for her taste. She finds a few funky pieces and puts together a couple of outfits to get her over until she can go out into the city. She phones her order down to the front desk in the lobby and surely enough the intercom buzzes a little less than an hour later. Cher lets the female attendant up on the elevator. She takes the packages in the foyer and then sends the neatly-dressed blonde back down on the elevator before opening the apartment door.

Once inside, Cher sets to tidying up. It is already one in the afternoon, so she decides not to go out shopping. She is afraid to miss Pharaoh's return at three. *There's always tomorrow for shopping*, she thinks while clearing the breakfast dishes from the table. Before she can set herself to any real progress, fatigue, like a noose, snuffs her off into sleep. She curls up on the sofa and drifts off into a dream.

****

John Rudolph Taylor, or *Rudy*, is there waiting for her. Cher hasn't seen him in years, not since she was nineteen. The sight of him catches her off guard, even in the dream.

If Cher has ever met with love, then Rudy was the man who introduced them. He was a young, White man with chestnut brown eyes and auburn hair. Cher met him one night at the Thoroughbred Lounge. With her burnt sienna skin, Cher was dark enough to pass for Black but too exotic to convince for long. She figured, off the top, that the only thing a White man could want with her was a little Lady Marmalade action.

Not to mention that Cher just didn't swing that way. She likes her men as strong and black as freshly-brewed coffee. If she was going to have a White man at all, it would have to be someone as funky as Harry "KC" Casey or as foxy as Robert Plant. Rudy wasn't even close. With his neat haircut, white-collared shirt and navy dress slacks, he looked like he just came from a board meeting. He was way too square and straight-laced for Cher's taste.

She wasn't taken with him initially, so she spurned him repeatedly, but his persistence eventually won her over. He came to the club three nights in a row before he could get her to speak to him. He bought her a ginger ale at the bar. Once Cher was sufficiently satisfied that he wanted nothing more than her company, she succumbed to his advances and joined him for dinner the following night.

They went to an expensive French restaurant. Cher partook of foods like *bouillabaisse* and *coq au vin*, the taste of which she only vaguely recalled from childhood memories of her mother. Everything was so lovely. The restaurant was dimly lit by candlelight that danced in Rudy's eyes. Cher was captivated by him. Rudy grew on her like a fungus. She couldn't help it. He was quite attractive with his long, thin nose and strong jaw. His light brown eyes were keen and seductive.

Rudy wined and dined her that night. They had a wonderful time: took in a show, did some gambling at the Stardust and afterwards sat by the fountains at Caesars Palace. They just talked on and on for what seemed like hours. Rudy's conversation was so eloquent and intellectual. He said he was a lobbyist and lived in Washington, DC. Cher didn't know what that was but it sure sounded important. Rudy invited her up to his room at the MGM Grand, but Cher declined his offer. This time his persistence did not triumph. Instead, she asked him to take her back to her apartment in Paradise.

After a steamy kiss, they said their goodbyes at her door. Cher spent the whole night, tossing in her bed and basting in sweat while clutching a pillow between her thighs. She fantasized about being a government wife and having dinner at the White House. The idea of it was overwhelmingly delightful. Cher found herself swept away on the prospect of where this affair could take her. She was absolutely positive that Rudy was taken with her and that their connection was more than just physical. He laid out so many details of his life to her that it was as though he was offering an invitation for her to come and join him there— in his life.

Cher got up early the next morning. Her mind was as restless as a toddler who needs a nap. She couldn't focus on anything, so she decided to go to her beautician. She got her hair pressed out straight and flowing to her hip like Cher Bono. She had her nails painted silver to match the funky platform shoes that she bought. Cher realized after it was all done that she was getting dolled up for Rudy. She wanted to believe it was just her way of pampering herself to pass the time; but the subconscious truth was that she hoped to see him again that night.

When Cher returned home, tired from her spree, Rudy rang her phone. She was excited to hear his voice at the other end of the line. He asked if she would take off work and spend his last night in town with him. Cher feigned hesitation, but then agreed after some intense groveling.

Rudy picked Cher up from her apartment and they headed out to the Hoover Dam. They sat in his robins-egg blue Plymouth Roadrunner convertible and watched the water rush down into the basin. The lights on the dam were so bright that the stars could not compete. Rudy told Cher about how he dreamed of becoming a senator some day when he was old enough. They were like Romeo and Juliet; young, star-crossed lovers finding each other across the great divide of race and class. Rudy didn't have to ask if she would spend his last night with him. Her body had already made its decision.

The valet at the MGM Grand took Rudy's keys, as he helped Cher out of the car. Cher began to feel that she could get used to this lifestyle. She received a few glares from some White, old-money tycoons in the lobby, but most who could not endure her presence simply turned a blind eye. By the time she reached Rudy's room, she was contemplating what his love would feel like. His hands were so warm on her shoulders when he slipped off her jacket. Rudy smiled deviously at Cher, as he led her across the salon of his suite to the bedchamber...

Long before the rays of the morning sun could shine through the windows and wake Cher, the sound of Rudy slipping back into his clothes did. Cher, feeling a sudden crisp chill in the air, wrapped herself in the sheets and sat up in the bed.

Rudy casually told her that he had an early flight back to Washington and could not stay any longer. She looked across the room and saw that his bags were already packed and sitting beside the door. Rudy told her that he enjoyed his time with her and if he ever came back to Vegas, he would look her up. Cher, stunned by the notion and tone of his *if*, asked if she was invited to visit him at the capital. To that question, Rudy simply replied that his wife and children might not appreciate it. He bid Cher a fair *adieu* and told her that she was welcome to stay in the room and order breakfast. He left two fifties on the bedside table.

Rudy disappeared from the door and took all trace of his

memory with him. As she dressed, Cher vigorously scrubbed her mind clean of every moment with him much the way she scrubbed the blood from her dress after the *procedure* to remove her stomach melons. She did such a good job eradicating all memory of Rudy that she didn't even recognize him, two months later, walking down the Vegas strip wearing an MGM Grand bellhop uniform. Cher decided then that love was for suckers. She hadn't even thought of Rudy from that day until now...

*There is Rudy in the flesh and waiting for Cher in her dreams. He sits on a bench in front of a pond with a fishing pole in his hand. Rudy thinks he has a tug, so he reels the line hard; tousling with the invisible force on the other end. He pulls relentlessly only to find that when he lifts the line from the water there is nothing on the hook. He does this two more times before he notices Cher watching him.*

*"What are you doing here, Rudy?" Cher asks quietly.*
*"Fishing-"*
*"Fishing for what?"*
*"Happiness," Rudy answers shortly, then turns back to the* pond.

Cher wakes suddenly, as if snatched out of the dream by an invisible hand. She wonders what the dream could mean. Because of her Creole bloodline, Cher is extremely superstitious about dreams and signs. She knew if she was dreaming of Rudy it had to mean something-

*But what?*

Cher did not know where she was or what awakened her

until the intercom buzzed a second time. She hops to her feet. Cher missed the sunset. It is already dark outside. She looks around, searching for the time. The clock above Pharaoh's television reads 7:10 pm. Cher curses herself for sleeping so long. She hurries out of the apartment and turns the key to release the elevator.

Minutes later Pharaoh and Musah arrive at the floor. Musah, a tall, broad-boned, dark-skinned Brother with a giant blowout afro, stays outside. When Pharaoh enters the apartment, he is visibly dismayed.

"Are you okay, Mama?" He looks into Cher's eyes, allowing the back of his hand to brush her cheek.

"I'm fine, Papa," she answers in benign dismissal.

"You sure you feeling alright?"

"Mmm hmm." She nods suspiciously. "Why do you ask?"

"When did I say I was coming back?"

"Three," Cher answers promptly.

"It's seven and you're still not dressed. Didn't I tell you we were going out to dinner tonight?"

"Yeah," Cher whines, pushing the toppled up do back from her forehead. "I guess I was so tired that I just fell asleep. I'm sorry."

"I will forgive this time," Pharaoh issues his pardon diplomatically. "I was worried about you when Musah told me that you didn't come down at all today."

"I didn't get my clothes until one and I didn't want to miss you at three, so I stayed and then I started to clean, but I-" Cher rambles off excuses, but Pharaoh cuts her short with a long, soft finger over her lips.

"I don't like to wait." The intensity is there again. Cher

cannot understand her attraction to Pharaoh. Is it living on the thin, dark edge of danger that excites her or is it the mystery of him? The secrets that his lips don't confess but his eyes reveal with clear expression.

"I'll be right back," Cher whispers sheepishly before scurrying into the bedroom.

Cher got ready faster than some would believe humanly possible. A few years as a dancer have made her an expert at changing quickly. A half-hour later, after a shower and a tiny act of God to get her hair looking decent, Cher emerges. She pulled her hair back in an elastic headband and let the poufy, tendrils drape down her back like a soft, curly Afro. She chose a pink and purple paisley midi dress and silver high heels with laces wound up around her calves to complete the ensemble. Cher pinched her cheeks to give them color and hoped that the few articles of makeup she kept in her purse– a tube of Pink Frost lipstick and a few eye shadows, were enough to make her sparkle for the night.

Pharaoh and Musah are seated in the living room engrossed in serious discussion when she steps out. If the look on their faces is any indication of her success, then Cher is ringing. Their conversation stops in mid-sentence and their mouths hang open. Musah quickly gathers his bearings and says lowly, in his deep Southern accent, "Pharaoh, I'll meet you downstairs."

Musah has a paranoid expression on his face as he slips from the room, but he doesn't need to worry. Pharaoh's eyes are glued firmly to Cher. Pharaoh probably wouldn't notice if the room was on fire, let alone any stray eyes checking out his filet. A shy smile of delight spreads across Pharaoh's face. He stands slowly and steps over to her. It's so endearing for Cher to watch him rub the sweat from his hands on his trousers before taking hold of hers.

"You look beautiful... like out of this world, Mama." He places a hand on his chest. "You knock me out." His smile, so childlike and sincere, makes Cher smile too. She earnestly hoped that his wait wouldn't sour the evening, but now she knows for sure that they are off to a good start.

"I made reservations for us at *La Dolce Vita* in Beverly Hills." Pharaoh helps Cher into her rabbit fur coat. "You will love this place. It's very upscale," he adds matter-of-factly. "Do you like Italian food?"

"That's just fine," Cher replies, looking over her shoulder at him. She can see the heat in his face when they make eye contact. He slips his arms into his own brown leather jacket, watching her the entire time. Cher can tell that Pharaoh is taken with her, more than he lets on. Pharaoh is cool now that he's older. He doesn't let passion take the lead anymore. Now every move he makes is the product of very careful deliberation.

"Let's go," he says, lightly placing his hand on the small of her back.

When Pharaoh and Cher reach the lobby, the doormen rush to open the glass doors for them like they are royalty. This is so different from the way that Cher is used to being treated. Being waited on by White people seems surreal, like an episode of that new television show "The Jeffersons".

Musah pulls up to the front of the building with Blaze in the passenger seat of a shimmering gold Chrysler Imperial. Cher didn't know that the sight of a car could bring her to the point of orgasm until that moment. Pharaoh opens the car door for Cher and climbs into the back seat with her. The valet closes the door and waves as they drive away.

Cher squirms in the seat, feeling giddy from the green velour interior under her thighs. "This car is so sick," Cher squeaks, running her hands over the soft upholstery. Pharaoh seems pleased that Cher is so impressed with his ride. He lays his right arm across the back of the seat behind Cher's head and places his left hand on her thigh. The heat from his hand travels and she begins to melt for him. Secretly, Cher is glad that she is wearing underwear tonight. She feels the squish of her juices. She would love for their first time to take place in the back of this luxury vehicle, but Cher doesn't want to put on a show for Pharaoh's associates in the front seat.

Pharaoh isn't nearly as affected by the small gesture of affection as Cher. He continues to stare past her out of the car window with a cautious expression. Cher remains quiet while they ride. She can feel Pharaoh's greatness as she sits beside him. She feels compelled to lay her head on his chest– so she does.

His body is warm against her cheek. Cher rests her hand on his stomach. Pharaoh responds to her touch, taking his eyes off the road and turning them to her for just a second. He rubs her shoulder and kisses her forehead.

"We're almost there, bunny." He pats her leg and then goes back to staring out of the window.

The Imperial climbs a long, stone driveway and emerges in front of a small building that looks as though it was carved out of the mountain rock which surrounds it. The restaurant is exquisite; dimly lit with small glass candle lamps on each white linen covered table. Shelves of expensive imported wines line the rough, stucco walls.

"I love it!" Cher exclaims, walking through the door that

Musah opens for them. The host takes their coats and they breeze past the other patrons who are waiting to be seated. Pharaoh steps aside and is met by the owner; a short, middle-aged Italian man, with shiny, Black hair and sharp dark eyes. Both men look intensely serious, speaking quietly to each other in Italian. Pharaoh makes big gestures with his hands. They both nod in agreement and then smiles break out on their faces.

"Si, Signore. Capisco," the man states simply, long lines stretch on his face as he grins and pats Pharaoh on the back.

"Grazie mille." Pharaoh shakes the man's hand sternly.

"Prego," the man replies sincerely, kissing his fingertips.

Pharaoh and Cher are escorted to a table in the rear of the restaurant- and not by the kitchen either, but right beside the large, glass windows that overlook the mountainside. They slide into a red-leather, circular booth. Musah and Blaze take their places in front of them, just inches away at a small table with high backed chairs. The two men sit on the edge of their seats and scan the room with fierce, militant eyes.

"Are they going to eat?" Cher asks curiously.

"No," Pharaoh answers shortly, unfolding a red linen napkin and placing it in Cher's lap.

"Do you take your men with you everywhere you go?"

"Yes." Pharaoh places a napkin in his lap and glances over at Cher. "You have a lot of questions."

Pharaoh rolls his eyes with irritation. Cher thinks that he may be upset with her inquisitiveness, so she settles into her seat and closes her mouth.

"You have lots of questions," he starts again. "but you are not asking what you really want to know." He smiles. "Do you find my men more interesting than me?" Pharaoh sits back and rests his long arms on top of the booth. His expression is stern, so Cher can't tell if he is offended or not.

"Of course not. You ringing, Boss." Cher gives him a seductive smile, bringing her cheek to her shoulder. Pharaoh checks her eyes to see if he is being played. When he's sure that Cher's compliment is sincere, his face softens and he takes her hand. He kisses her palm softly. Cher has to squeeze her thighs together to put out the fire that his lips ignited.

"I wasn't sure if I could ask personal questions," Cher says with a tone of embarrassment.

"You can ask me anything you like, Mama. I want you to know me and I want to get to know you too. I brought you out to my crib, so I want you to feel as safe in my den as I do. That starts by knowing with whom you live, right?"

Cher feels the apprehension drain from her body. She didn't realize that she was so uptight around him. Cher wonders if Pharaoh can feel the tension too. All the same, she is glad to see the wall between them breaking down.

"Let's rap, baby. Ask your questions." He smiles, covering her hand on the table with his.

"Righteous," she peeps enthusiastically. Cher feels the same as when he gave her the credit card– overwhelmed by his generosity. She can tell that Pharaoh is a very private man so it makes her feel special to have this intimacy with him. Her nipples stiffen, as the thought of physical intimacy enters her meditation.

"How old are you?"

Pharaoh huffs a tiny laugh at the simplicity of her first question. Cher is cute to him. He expected hard-hitting, investigative questions from her, but instead she is treating this dinner like a true first date. She acts casual, as though she isn't already living in his pad with him.

"Okay," he replies passively, rubbing his palms together. "I'm thirty-one... as of today, actually."

"Awww," Cher exclaims excitedly. "It's your birthday," she peeps. Pharaoh nods with a soft, pleasant smile. "Why didn't you tell me? I would have gotten *you* a gift."

"You are my gift," he whispers. "I like to pick out my own presents and you are what I chose."

Blood rushes to Cher's face and she can't help but blush. Pharaoh stares at her intensely. She feels light-headed and her temples begins to throb. She would have thought it was from the seduction of his words, but the light grumbling in her stomach indicates otherwise.

"Can we order now?"

"Any and every thing you want." Pharaoh lifts his hand to summon the waiter.

A young, dark haired Italian boy comes promptly to the table with a notepad. Cher points to items on the menu and Pharaoh explains to her what the words mean. Once she finds what she likes, Pharaoh commands the boy (in seemly effortless Italian) to bring it out, "Pronto."

"Si Signore," the boy answers with respect.

"So do you speak many languages?"

"Yes." Pharaoh pours Cher a glass of wine. "I speak the languages of my business associates: Spanish, Italian, and even some Chinese."

Cher refuses the wine. "No thank you. I don't drink," she says politely. Pharaoh is a little taken aback, but then shrugs and places the glass in front of himself.

"Is that why you speak with an accent?"

"I didn't know I had an accent," he replies with sincere surprise. "No one has ever told me that before."

"Straight up," Cher says, leaning forward. "It comes and goes, but I find it strange because I thought you were Black."

"I am," he answers with pride.

"But not completely, I'm sure." Cher discerns intuitively.

"My mother was Cuban and my father was African. Does that answer your question?" Pharaoh responds, seemingly agitated by the admission.

"Did your mother teach you Spanish?" Cher asks eagerly.

"My mother did not teach me anything." A tinge of anger seeps into his tone. "She abandoned my father and me. I was raised in Long Beach with Blacks. I am a Brother. That's the only family I know. I learned Spanish from the Eses in my neighborhood; but like I said, that was business-related."

Cher feels like she stepped on Pharaoh's foot, so she tries to repair the breach.

"Me... I'm Creole. My father was French and African and mother was Haitian and Indian. So I speak a little French, just what ma mere taught me before she died."

Pharaoh smiles. The anxiety about his mother drains from his face. "Now that's pretty special." He caresses her chin. "There's a language I don't know. Would you teach me?" He asks with childlike eagerness.

"Oui, Papa. Quoi que tu souhaites." Cher answers, lowering her lids. "Whatever you wish."

Something about the way she breathes the words turns Pharaoh on. His manhood stiffens. He likes to hear her talk that way; but at the same time, it makes him suspicious. Pharaoh doesn't trust women. His mother packing up and walking out on him caused him to be that way. He figured if you can't even trust your own mother, then what woman can you trust. But with Cher, it is different. He knows he can train her and (maybe one day) possibly even come to love and trust her. Then again, Pharaoh had seen it go wrong time and time again with women. In his mind, they are unpredictable and treacherous creatures. To Pharaoh, loving a woman was about like sleeping with an alligator. He just knew they were bound to turn on him eventually. As for Cher, he would just have to wait and see.

The food comes out quickly and they begin to eat. It takes three waiters to dress their table. Lasagna, fettuccini, linguine and a host of other dishes that Cher couldn't pronounce were placed before them.

*This is quite a spread*, Cher thinks to herself. She has never seen so much food on one table before; except for once when one of her foster families had a barbeque and invited all of their family. Cher had no other basis for comparison, so she figured that Pharaoh was inviting her into his family.

"This is my first time seeing you eat. I didn't think that you did– eat or sleep, I mean. You're just too good to be true."

Pharaoh doesn't take compliments from women well, but he doesn't let it show in his conversation.

"Well, I'm flesh and blood, baby." Pharaoh lifts his hands and turns them front to back. Cher giggles nervously. She longs to feel his large, soft hands on her body, but she doesn't want to be too forward. Pharaoh is definitely a man who likes to be in control; plus having an audience in Musah and Blaze keeps Cher cool.

After eating their fill and leaving more food on the table than they consumed, Pharaoh and Cher leave the restaurant. Cher is careful to make note that Pharaoh never paid for anything. They just got up and walked out to the nods and grins of the employees.

"Grazie di tutto," Pharaoh says, throwing up a hand before exiting the door.

His power... his authority... his status turns Cher on so much that she can hardly contain herself when he slides into the back seat beside her. Don't get it wrong- Pharaoh is fine to look at, but something about a man who can snap his fingers and manifest his desires is more than a woman like Cher is used to. Cher crosses her right leg over her left and lets it come to rest on Pharaoh's knee.

Pharaoh lifts an eyebrow at her forwardness, but he lets it ride. He is feeling her pretty tough too. Pharaoh slides his hand along the outside of her thigh and until it slips under her dress. He squeezes the warm, plump flesh at her hip. Cher sighs so heavily that it catches the attention of Musah and Blaze, who are too intimidated to dare take a look in the rearview mirror. They continue on, eyes focused ahead, as though they hear nothing.

Pharaoh kisses Cher. Public displays of affection are strictly prohibited for him. It's unprofessional in his mind, but he has already broken the rule once with her, so the second time feels even better. Her lips are soft on his. She sucks gently on his bottom lip and Pharaoh feels his manhood begin to throb. That is enough for him. He knows he can't go there with her, so he stops. Pharaoh puts her leg back where it belongs. He pulls her hands from around his neck and places them in her lap.

"Pump your brakes, Mama," he says quietly, then begins to stare out of his own car window again. He wouldn't even look at her after that. His gesture upsets Cher. She can't understand his rejection. She hopes that he doesn't think ill of her. She realizes that he did meet her in a strip club, so she hopes that he doesn't think she's easy after that display. Cher is half-afraid that he might even throw her out of his apartment when they get back.

"I had intended to show you my city, tonight," Pharaoh states mildly, still staring out of his window. "But it's later than I expected, so would you mind if we retire for the evening?"

Cher shakes her head nervously. *This can't be good?* She thinks to herself, as they pull up in front of his building. When they step inside of the red-carpeted elevator, Cher puts the key into the board and presses the 14 button. She watches his mannerisms in the panel mirrors the entire way up. Pharaoh stares at the ground and rubs the back of his neck. He seems nervous and insecure, not like at the restaurant. Cher turns the lock and Pharaoh opens the apartment door, motioning for her to come inside.

Cher steps across the threshold. Pharaoh is kind. He helps Cher out of her coat and hangs it in the closet. He stands behind her and kisses her neck before going upstairs to his den. Cher feels so rejected at first, but then she decides to put it out of her mind.

*Maybe Pharaoh has some business to finish upstairs and will be back down shortly.*

She goes into his bedroom and tidies the satin sheets, pulling the soft, down duvet up over the pillows. She arranges the bead strings on the canopy over his circular bed to look undisturbed. She wants everything to be perfect for him when he joins her in the bedroom tonight. She goes into the bathroom and freshens up for him. Cher brushes her teeth. She changes the underwear soaked with her feminine fluids and puts on a black lace thong. She ordered a peek-a-boo, black-lace nighty from Macy's to match. She slips into it, so that Pharaoh can see her full, round breasts. The feeling of the lace brushing against her large, throbbing nipples makes her ache for his touch. Once Cher is sure she looks stunning, she steps out of the bathroom, but Pharaoh isn't waiting in the bedroom. She walks out into the living room but he isn't there either. Cher pauses at the bottom of the spiral staircase. She takes the first five steps and then calls up to him.

"Come on up, Mama." He answers faintly.

When she comes to the top of the stairs, light pours from beneath the door on the left, so she approaches. Pharaoh is replacing large binders on a shelf at the back of the room, when she enters. The room is huge and obviously doubles as a home office, with a grand desk and a large, brown leather chair in its center. Each wall is lined with shelves of books. Cher takes note of them- some of which she would not expect a man like Pharaoh to read: War and Peace, Crime and Punishment, even Pride and Prejudice. His library is quite extensive. The room has wood paneling on the walls and a big African print throw rug over the carpet. A few expensive looking chairs and a long leather sofa are positioned comfortably throughout the den. The high glass ceiling slants, but still leaves ample room for a man as tall as Pharaoh to be comfortable walking around in the space. The melody of a record spinning on his player finds her ears. "Could It Be I'm Falling in Love," by The Spinners is one of Cher's favorites. She is captivated by the music. She desperately wants to move... to dance even, but she contains herself, satisfied only to have Pharaoh's attention.

She studies him as he stretches to put the binders up on a high shelf. His is shirtless, wearing only a pair of navy cotton shorts. His body is more muscular than she would have expected for his slender frame. He is nicely-built with a thin layer of curly hair that covers his chest and stomach. When Pharaoh finally turns around to see her, he is awe-struck. It's not too often that Pharaoh gets excited about a fox, especially since he's had so many, but Cher caught him off guard. He hasn't had a woman in his crib for years, so he doesn't get *The Special Treatment* every day. The care that Cher put into preparing herself for him takes his breath away. He surveys her body. Her firm brown nipples poking against the gown arouse him. Pharaoh is speechless and Cher is delighted by the expression on his face. A man as stoic as Pharaoh can hide the way he feels, but he can't hide the huge erection that struggles against the fabric of his shorts. The sound of the binder in his hand hitting the floor, snaps him back to reality.

"Hey, Cher. Come here, Mama." His tone is concerned. She steps away from the door and takes his outstretched hand. "Sit down with me." Pharaoh takes a seat in a brown armchair and pats his lap. Cher sits down and feels the thick, pulsing flesh of his manhood against her thigh. He breathes her in deeply, putting his face into the hair that lies around her neck. He pecks a tiny, soft kiss on her collarbone. "You don't think this is why I brought you here, do you?"

Cher finds the question strange. She doesn't know how she is supposed to answer it. Pharaoh sees the confusion in her face.

"This is **not** why I brought you here. You are more to me than this." He gently rubs her smooth thighs.

"I don't understand you," Cher says, feeling the heat drain from her body. She begins to cool and goose bumps appear on her arms. "Don't you want me?"

"Oh yes," he answers earnestly, pecking kisses on her lips. "Don't doubt that, Mama. You are fly and foxy, but I want you in many ways and for many reasons not just this one." He lays his head on her shoulder. Cher strokes his hair. It's longer and softer than it looks from the way he wears it slicked back behind his ears.

"Pharaoh never takes anything that isn't rightfully his." He looks into her eyes. "Pharaoh does not accept anything that is given, only that which he has won... only that which he has conquered." He rubs her arm and pats her hand like a father.

"But I am yours, Papa." Cher turns her hip and lays her thigh across his lap, straddling him. To hell with being forward, she wants Pharaoh and she wants him to know that she does.

"You won me, Daddy." She kisses him deeply and he allows her to. He submerges his hands into her hair and tastes her mouth with his tongue. Cher spreads her hands wide on his chest and presses her love against his package. She can feel tiny waves of pleasure radiating through her hips.

"Mmm– Wait Cher." Pharaoh grabs her wrists before she can plunge her hands into his shorts. "I'm an intelligent man. I see the reservations that you think you're hiding from me," he states, brushing her hair away from her face. "I know you're afraid of me and for good reason. You don't even know me, but that's okay. We've got time. I'm not going to bed you until I know that I can trust you and you know that you can trust me with your life." Pharaoh kisses her so gently that her heart breaks. "Alright, my filet?"

"Alright," she breathes on his lips. Cher sighs her resignation as Pharaoh presses her up into a standing position. He rises from the armchair and follows her to the door of the den. He smacks her butt cheek hard, as he watches her walk in front him.

Cher looks over her shoulder to see him biting down on his lip. "I apologize." He raises his hands in surrender. "I couldn't resist it, Mama. That thing looks so *fine*," Pharaoh hisses.

He hugs her tightly, pressing her head against his chest, and then kisses her once more before sending her back down the stairs alone. Only the melody follows her into the bedroom.

*"Could it be I'm falling in love... with you... with you-"*

# CITY OF ANGELS

"Good morning, bunny," Pharaoh says cheerfully, pecking a tiny kiss on Cher's cheek when she enters the kitchen in his plain, white T-shirt. He runs his hands roughly over her frazzled hair, as a playful gesture. Cher smiles and wraps her arms around his waist, pressing up on her toes to place a heavy kiss on his lips.

"Did you sleep well?" He asks, looking down on her.
"Not hardly," she answers dismally.

Cher would never admit it to Pharaoh, but she spent most of the night tossing on his mattress like the Princess and the Pea. She burned so passionately for Pharaoh that she wasn't able to rest until she had pleasured herself... a few times. Cher laid in his bed and imagined his body on hers while she brought herself to climax under his covers. Cher felt ashamed of the loneliness that she felt when she rolled over to sleep without him. Pharaoh was making his way into her heart so quickly that it scared her. As much as she hated the way he turned her down physically, Cher was glad that they hadn't crossed that line yet. If his kiss is any indication of what his love feels like, then Cher would definitely be hooked on him.

Pharaoh hands Cher a plate of toast and eggs with bacon, then leaves the kitchen. Cher carries the plate over to the table. She would never have imagined that Pharaoh would be the kind of man to wait on his woman like this, but here he is making her breakfast yet another morning.

"Cher honey," Pharaoh calls from his bedroom doorway.
"Yeah Papa." She jumps up from the table and comes into the room. Cher watches Pharaoh dress and is grateful to be a witness to it. It's like he is transforming into a prince right before her eyes. He slides a cream colored turtleneck over his head, and it hugs his body the way Cher wants to; showing off

his tight, muscular chest. Pharaoh steps into a pair of brown suede bell-bottoms, then takes off his bandana and heads into the bathroom to brush his hair.

"I want you to take the right side of the closet. Put all of my things on the left, okay?" Pharaoh says, draping a thick, gold chain with an ankh medallion around his neck.

"I can dig it." Cher nods.

"Musah is taking you out to get your hair and nails done today. You have an eleven o'clock appointment at Frenchie's Salon on Ventura Boulevard. Then you can go wherever you want after that." He fastens the clasps on his gold bracelets and presses gold rings on the middle, ring and pinky fingers of his left hand.

"Okay," Cher answers shortly, crossing her arms over her chest.

"What's wrong, Mama?" Pharaoh stops short of putting on his Italian leather platform shoes. He comes over to rub her shoulders. Cher finds it bizarre how responsive he is to her needs. On the surface, Pharaoh didn't seem to be that type of man.

"I just want to spend some time alone with you today," she pleads.

"Really now," Pharaoh says with an eyebrow raised. "Is that what you want?"

"Mmm hmm," Cher nods like an eager little girl.

"Well, I have a meeting this morning that I cannot miss, but I tell you what-" Pharaoh pauses, tapping the tip of her nose. "I think I can clear the afternoon for my filet. Will that suffice?"

Cher nods anxiously, biting on her bottom lip.

"Okay, well you go and get all foxy for me and I'll pick you up from the salon when you're done."

Cher half-expected that Pharaoh would not show up that afternoon since his three turned into seven yesterday, but Pharaoh arrived at the salon a little after two, just as she was getting the final touches put on her nails. The employees in the salon treat Pharaoh like a celebrity when he comes through the door. The attendants anxiously ask if he needs anything, circling around him like lap dogs. But Pharaoh dismisses them with a wave of his hand, focusing all of his attention on Cher– who defies the beauty he thought she was capable of achieving. Cher looks to him like she stepped off of a movie screen or out of a magazine, in her burgundy-colored coolot pants and flowing, pink chiffon tunic. Pharaoh runs his fingers through her hair, which had been pressed out to silky, shiny perfection. His hands follow the soft strands until they end just above the small of her back.

"Solid," he breathes in amazement.
"You like it, Papa?" Cher asks seductively.
"Oh yeah. Out of sight, Mama."

Pharaoh and Cher walk out of the salon to his Coupe Deville parked at the curb. Pharaoh didn't so much as put a hand in his pocket, let alone pay for anything before they left. He simply breezed out to the car and opened the passenger door for Cher before climbing into the driver's seat next to her.

"Just you and me, Papa?"
"Just me and you." He shrugs with a smile. "Where do you want to go?"
"Anywhere you want to take me." Cher beams, wrapping her

hand around his elbow.

A few short minutes later, they arrive in Long Beach. Cher is shocked because she thought that Pharaoh's life was all glitz and glamour. For him to take her there didn't quite fit with her image of him. Graffiti, which covers the sides of the buildings they pass, is the only vibrant color in the community: no glass, no steel here- just concrete.

Even the park is full of concrete: no grass, no trees– just concrete. The Brothers, with cornrows and afros, are juking on the basketball courts, playing the game as if it is their last. A few females sit nearby on the bleachers in denim mini-skirts, popping gum and cheering loudly for their men.

"Where are we going?"

"It's a surprise," Pharaoh replies passively.

A few minutes more and Pharaoh turns his car into a neighborhood called Inglewood. He pulls up in front of a small, blue house and kills the engine. Two young, dark-skinned boys sit on the curb at the corner of the house. Pharaoh approaches them.

"Hey lil' Brothers. What it be like?" Pharaoh gives them a funky handshake. "I need you to do me a big favor."

"Sure Mistah." The little boy smiles, one of his front teeth missing.

"Watch this car." Pharaoh points. "If anyone comes near it, you knock on that door right there, okay?"

"Okay." The boy nods, squinting from the sun that surrounds Pharaoh's face.

"Solid, lil' man." Pharaoh gives him a ten-dollar bill. The boy's eyes widen and he stuffs it quickly into his pocket. He

begins to watch the car like a pit bull and Pharaoh grins at his
instant vigilance.

"Come on, Cher." Pharaoh takes her hand, as if more for
possession than affection. They climb the three steps to the
porch of the house and Pharaoh knocks on the screen door.

"Who is it?" a thin, shrill voice screeches.
"It's me Big Mama," Pharaoh calls loudly through the door.
"Is that you, Mason?"
"Yeah it's me."

A tiny, elderly dark-skinned woman answers the door. She is
stooped over, but still moves around well in a powder blue
housecoat. Her course white hair is braided down into three long
plaits.

"Oh Mason," she squeals, lifting her hands to hug him.
Pharaoh bends low, so the small woman can kiss his cheek. Her
hand is heavy when she pats his shoulder. "Who 'dis pretty girl
ya' got witcha?"

"Big Mama, this is Cher," he says dropping his head to walk
through the doorway. Cher follows Pharaoh into the house. It's
a small, cluttered residence with piles of old newspapers stacked
on the scuffed hardwood floors in the living room. The scent of
moth balls and analgesic balm hangs heavy in the air.

"Ain't you just a pretty young thang?" Big Mama holds
Cher's arms out to inspect her. "How old is you, sweetheart?"
"I'm twenty-one, ma'am."
"Oh no, don't call me ma'am. Call me Big Mama like
Mason do."
Cher smiles at the use of Pharaoh's first name. She thinks it

is so charming to find out that Pharaoh was once someone's little *Mason*.

"Y'all have a seat," she squeaks anxiously.

"I just came to check up on you Big Mama, but I can't stay long." Pharaoh returns to a little boy around this woman. It's yet another side of Pharaoh that Cher didn't see coming. He sits on the flowery, plastic-covered couch and pats the cushion for Cher to come and sit next to him.

"Y'all want something to drank?"

"No Big Mama," Pharaoh answers cordially, as she slowly lowers herself down into her yellow recliner.

"Well, Mason," she says, making small talk. "The doctor say my blood pressure is down and my heart looking real good these days."

"That's great news. I'm glad you've been taking care of yourself."

"Well, that nurse aide you got coming every day is helping me to keep up with my diet and my medicines. Thank you again, Sugar." The s in each word whistles against her toothless gums.

"Anything for you." He touches his heart and sits forward in the chair. "I really want you to think about that community that I want to put you up in– the one out in Beverly Hills. They got a lot of senior programs and shopping-"

"Mason, if I told you once, then I told you a thousand times. I'm not leaving Long Beach. This is my home. My husband and my son is buried here." She sucks on her gums and the irritation of this familiar subject shows on her face.

"You can come see them anytime you want. I'll hire a driver to take you *anywhere* you want to go, *anytime* you want to go."

"That's your lifestyle and I don't judge it, so now let this old woman have hers." She pats her chest, but never looks him in the eye. Cher can see, as she listens to his grandmother, where Pharaoh gets his stubborn streak from. "I'm staying in Long Beach and you welcome to come and visit me as much as you like, but I won't be leaving, baby."

"Okay, Big Mama," he sighs, conceding to her. "You know I love you, right?"

"I love you too Mason."

The little boy knocks on the screen door. "Hey Mistah, they a man standing by yo' car."

Pharaoh walks over and looks out at the curb. "It's cool lil' man. Good looking out." Pharaoh opens the screen door and steps out on the porch. "Cher, stay here with Big Mama for a minute while I take care of some business." Cher nods and Pharaoh walks out to the street.

"Sugar, you sho' is pretty. You 'mind me o' Mason's mama. You know that?" The tiny woman stares Cher directly in her eyes. The loose skin around Big Mama's eyes hangs in bags. The deep wrinkles on her face tell a long, sad story like hieroglyphic carvings on the walls of a pyramid. Big Mama looks tired, but it's that kind of weariness that comes from the vexation of the spirit, more than the aging of the body.

"Thank you, Big Mama," Cher replies courteously.

"I'ma talk to you like I would one of my own chi'ren." Her tone is secretive like she is in a confessional booth with Cher. "If you know what's good for you chile', you'll leave my Mason alone."

Her words hit Cher like a punch to the chest. She expected this woman to have glowing remarks about her grandson. Cher would never expect to hear about a man from his own flesh and blood. Cher was on the verge of believing that Pharaoh was such a good man, she couldn't imagine what Big Mama could be talking about.

"Mason is a good man... a good man, I tell you." Big Mama shakes her head and her eyes moisten. Cher begins to wonder if Big Mama is lucid. She wants to dismiss the woman as senile, but she can't help herself. She has to listen. Something in Big Mama's eyes tells Cher that she knows what she is talking about.

"My son, Kingston– Mason's father, was a good man too; strong and a real good provider, but too sensitive. He beat Mason's mama, Desola, something awful for every little thing she did wrong. If she burned dinner, or broke a dish, or came home late, he would unleash such violence on her."

"Now Desola truly loved my Kingston. She stuck in there with him. Even though she shouldn't have, she probably would have stayed with him. But when Mason got old enough to know what was happening, she didn't want him to grow up seeing what his daddy was doing to her. When she told King that she was leaving him and taking Mason with her, it was more than he could bear. I didn't see Desola no more after that." Big Mama drops her eyes to her lap.

"King told us that she left him and went back to Cuba with her parents. But I knowed that was a lie 'cause she wouldn't never leave Mason with Kingston." Big Mama's eyes dart across the room.

"Mason ain't been right neither. His daddy filled him full of poison with them stories about his mama abandoning them. I tried to tell Mason that Desola wouldn't just leave him and that something must have happened to her, but he wouldn't believe me. His daddy was all he had and King was like a god to

79

Mason. His word was the only one that Mason would accept."
A look of guilt comes over Big Mama's face and she wrings her
hands. "I love Mason. I truly do. He ain't like his daddy. He got
a kind, soft heart- but he got the devil in him, too. When he was
ten years old, I seen him beat a kid damn near to deaf over two
dollars. I ain't never seen that kind of rage in no chile'. I'ma
only tell you once to be careful, 'cause I don't know what my
grandbaby is capable of."

Big Mama sits back in her chair and crosses her hands across
her lap. She looks serene, pleasant even, when Pharaoh comes
back through the door. It is only the look on Cher's face that
gives away the gravity which took place in that room minutes
earlier.

"What's wrong, Cher?" Mason asks tenderly.
"Oh nothing. I just got a headache, that's all," Cher lies,
gripping her head. She tries so hard to play off what she just
heard. Cher is terrified and it shows on her face.
"Alright, bunny." Pharaoh rubs Cher's shoulder. "I do
apologize. You probably just need a bite to eat. It is almost
dinner time." Pharaoh bends down to his Big Mama and gives
her a peck on her cheek. "I'll be back to check on you later this
week, alright?"
"Alright, Mason baby." She pinches his cheeks with her
withered hands. She smiles at him so brightly that the shadow of
all she just said seems to disappear.
"Come on Cher." He reaches for her hand. "Catch you later,
Big Mama."

She waves them out and locks the door behind them. Thick
iron bars cover all the windows, making Big Mama look like a

prisoner in her house, as she watches through the curtains.

"Why did you take me to meet your Big Mama?" Cher asks quietly. Long strands of hair whip across her face when Pharaoh drops the convertible top. Pharaoh puts on his dark, Ray Ban aviator sunglasses.

"Because she is the only woman that I will ever love more than you." His eyes are focused on the road, but she can feel the sincerity of his words. "Do you know how many of my women have met Big Mama?"

Cher shakes her head.

"One," he answers bluntly. "Her name is Cher." His jaw clenches. "Do you know why that is?"

"No," Cher replies nervously.

"Because I've never been *in* love before-" Pharaoh suddenly pulls the car off the road and comes to a halt on the side of the highway. "Big Mama is the only woman I've ever believed really loved me– who loved me enough for me to trust her."

Cher swallows hard, realizing that Pharaoh doesn't know his trust is in vain.

"I want that with you... something that I've never had with a woman before. I need to know that I can trust you, that you won't leave me. No one knows what it's like to be alone in this world because you can't trust anybody." Cher cannot see his eyes, but she can feel his pain. She knows that brand of loneliness and empathizes with him.

Cher thinks about Big Mama's warning, but then realizes that she hadn't actually said anything bad about Pharaoh. Maybe if he could trust her, then she could change him. Pharaoh does have a gentle heart and even Big Mama had to acknowledge that.

"I know it's only been a couple of days, but I'm falling hard for you Cher." Pharaoh places his hand on her thigh. Cher is amazed by his words. She had no idea his feelings were as strong as hers. "The way I feel about you is making me soft. I think about you all day long. I can't get you off my mind. It's even affecting my work." Pharaoh hangs his head. "Having you here is heavier than I thought it would be. I don't think I can continue on this way with you, not knowing if you're going to stay."

Pharaoh is more vulnerable with Cher than she knew he was capable of. This man of stone is crumbling before her very eyes and placing the pieces in her hands. "I'd rather end this now and send you back to your life in Vegas, if I can't trust you... if I can't have you completely to myself." Pharaoh takes off his shades. His dark eyes are red and moist.

How could Cher refuse him?

If she thought that his power and his status were magnetic, then his sensitivity is even more compelling.

"Well, Pharaoh, I-" Cher begins hesitantly.

"Say no more, ma cherie," Pharaoh interrupts, waving his hand. "I will give you the day- the rest of this day with me to make a decision. In the morning, you can either go back to Vegas with Blaze, or you can stay in L.A. with me."

Pharaoh's eyes are tender. He makes himself small, curving his shoulders down, as he kisses Cher's fingertips. "I told you last night that I want to show you my city. We still have many hours in the day to make good on my plans." Pharaoh leans over to kiss her. Cher can tell that his kiss is different, more delicate and defenseless than before. His lips tremble a bit when they press against hers.

"Let's beat the drag, foxy." Pharaoh replaces his sunglasses and speeds away.

****

Their next stop is Santa Monica. Pharaoh takes Cher to a tiny *bodega* situated near a pier. Cher wonders the reason for the visit, but soon realizes when they walk through the door.

"Aye... Que pasa!" Several voices exclaim when Pharaoh enters the store. A couple of older Mexican women rush to Pharaoh and embrace him.

"Como estas, Mijo?" The lady kisses his cheeks. She feels along his arm. "Por que tan flaco?" she asks with hands on her hips and a deep frown in her brows.

"Si, si. Yo se, Mami." He smiles and presses his hands together like in prayer. "Cocinara para mi, por favor?"

"Por supuesto, Flaco." She smiles at him and pats his cheek. "Venga, Papi."

Cher had no idea what the exchange was about until they were led into a kitchen attached to a tiny apartment in the back of the store.

"Sientese," the woman says, pointing towards a tiny redwood table with two metal lawn chairs on either side. The small space is clean but meager with flower wallpaper and green linoleum flooring. Cher isn't sure she wants to eat there once she realizes that a meal is being prepared. But Pharaoh continues to smile and make small talk with the woman while she pulls pots from underneath the sink. He seems so comfortable that Cher doesn't want to appear unappreciative.

"Aye Ese!" Two short, husky men remark, as they come into the kitchen through the back door. Both of them have a dark olive complexions and thick, greased dark hair. The younger of the two wears a long braid down his back. "They told us that Pharaoh was here, but we couldn't believe it until we saw it for ourselves. What's happening, Holmes?"

Pharaoh rises from the table and shares a familial handshake with the men. They laugh and seem genuinely excited to see him. Cher wonders if they are his family but she doesn't ask, recalling his offense from the night before.

"What brings you out to Santa Monica, man? We don't see you hanging around these parts no more." The young man tucks his thumbs into the front pockets of his denim pants and leans against the counter.

"I'm just here with my lady to get some of your aunt's out-of-this-world cooking." Pharaoh pats the woman's shoulder as she carries a large pot from the stove to the sink. "You know you'll never keep me away from Santa Monica as long as she is here."

Cher made a note that neither of the other two men glanced at her once. They didn't even acknowledge her presence. She thought it was strange but maybe cultural, so she paid it no mind. She just sat in her seat, being unwilling seduced by the scrumptious aroma of onions and chili peppers that filled the tiny kitchen.

"Cher baby." Pharaoh snaps to get her attention. Cher had been ignored for so long that she was beginning to think she was invisible. "I need to handle some business with Alejandro and Lito. I'll be right back, okay?" Pharaoh waits for Cher to nod her approval before leaving the kitchen with the two men.

The older lady continues to cook away during his absence. She wields plump hands, with dimples where the knuckles should be, like paintbrushes creating a masterpiece on the canvas of her stove. She moves quickly and skillfully, dicing up a handful of tomatoes in the blink of an eye; then scattering them into the simmering pot. She rubs her hands briskly on the clean white apron tied around her waist, then wipes the sweat from her brow with the back of her chubby forearm. Cher can tell this woman cooks from a very passionate place. This woman has established her worth with this craft and her pride shows in the simplest things, like the way she sprinkles her seasonings into each steaming pot. She seems to create some deep, spiritual incantation as she stirs. She whips the giant, wooden spoon around in a large vat of black beans, spiced with tomatoes and red peppers. She smiles a deep internal satisfaction when she turns the stove knobs to off. In seemingly no time at all, she asks Cher to help her serve the plates.

"Ayudeme, Mija," she pipes sweetly, handing Cher two platter-style plates, loaded down so heavy with food that Cher's arms dip under their weight. The short, round woman hobbles on broad, stocky legs over to the screen door and yells across the way. "Venga! La comida esta lista!"

The men come rushing in for dinner like school boys. Cher smiles to see the excitement on Pharaoh's face, as he rubs his hands together and kisses the woman's cheek. She points to the plate with the most food and smacks his shoulder. Pharaoh sits on the left, Cher on the right and the woman, bringing a chair from the *bodega*, sits in the middle. She takes their hands and

Pharaoh bows his head, showing respect for her custom. She recites the grace and everyone in the kitchen, save Cher– who did not know the prayer was over, says "Amen" and crosses their chests.

Alejandro and Lito take their plates and lean against the counter. It is tight in the kitchen but more because of the love that bursts from the seams than the bodies present. The men devour the food heartily, using the thick, pillowy flour tortillas like spoons to shovel mounds of rice, beans and corn into their mouths. They joke and laugh with each other, enchanted by the mirth of the food. The older lady is quietly delighted to see their enjoyment. Her eyes twinkle while she watches Pharaoh eat.

The food is savory. Cher has never before tasted anything quite like it. Her favorite item is the beans, which melt in her mouth. Each delicious bite bursts with rich flavor as if all of the spices are contained within tiny bubbles. Cher would have been content to end her meal halfway into her plate, just one of the Frisbee-sized tortillas satisfied her appetite. But as she slows, the older lady pats her shoulder.

"Coma...coma!" She smiles. "Es tan flaca tambien."

Pharaoh winks at Cher and the other men laugh along. Two teenage girls enter the kitchen and fall on Pharaoh, hugging him tightly around his neck. After the fuss dies down, the girls prepare plates for themselves and another for an elderly man who comes shuffling into the tiny kitchen behind them. The girls lean against the doorframe and Pharaoh rises from his seat, offering it to the older man. Pharaoh kisses the man's cheek as he sits down in the chair. The man covers the hand that Pharaoh places on his shoulder with his own withered hand and gazes up at him with gratitude.

Cher realizes, looking around the small room, that this is her

Pharaoh- her *Mason*. He values family and relationships, trust and respect. Again Pharaoh has set a table before her, inviting her into his family. As Pharaoh gazes at her from across the room, catching her in his seductive stare; Cher can tell in that very moment that his feelings for her are solid. His eyes, which remain constant on her even while the others are talking to him, show the truth– that she has gotten under his skin. She is in his head and in his heart.

"Muchas gracias," Pharaoh says, grasping Cher's hand after the meal and leading her out the back door of the bodega. Cher notes that for the first time, Pharaoh did offer money in exchange for a service. He rolled off a few bills for the older lady, but she popped his shoulder with a long wooden spoon, offended at the prospect of taking his money.

"Algo para ti, Mijo," she says, kissing Pharaoh's cheek before he disappears out of the door.

"You just ate the **best** food in Southern California. Hands down."

"I can dig it, Papa." Cher nods with smile, flipping her hair behind her shoulder. "It was definitely ringing. I've never tasted anything like it in my life."

"Well that's what I want... to introduce you to things you've never experienced before," Pharaoh says quietly, taking her hand without looking at her.

Pharaoh and Cher walk slowly along the boardwalk out towards the beach. A dull, gray twilight is falling around them. Cher takes off her beaded scandals and lets the cold, gritty sand squish between her toes. Even though Santa Monica in late December is definitely not a tropic island in the Pacific, Cher still enjoys the experience of feeling the sea spray on her skin and listening to the sound of the waves crashing against the shore. The leaves of the palm trees wave an excited "hello" at the unction of a cool sea breeze which blows through them. Pharaoh refuses to remove any article of his clothing and walks along the shore in his expensive Italian leather shoes. Cher rolls up the legs of her coolot pants and tip-toes out into the water. She shrieks when the first tiny waves slap against her calves, sending water splashing up into her face.

Pharaoh laughs. "It's cold, hunh?" He calls to her over the rushing surf.

"Is this what you call cold?" Cher huffs confidently. Cher doesn't care. She relishes the sensation of her feet slipping down into the sand deeper and deeper as each wave, swirls around her ankles and carries away a little more of the foundation. Pharaoh watches her spin in the water, mesmerized by her movements as if those of a beautiful sea nymph.

"Come out of there! Your clothes are getting wet and I don't want you catching pneumonia," Pharaoh shouts gruffly.

"Don't be such a square, Papa. I've never been to a beach before." She lifts her arms over her head and hops with each wave. The wispy sleeves of her tunic waft on the wind, transforming Cher into an earth angel with beautiful pink butterfly wings.

"Really?" Pharaoh asks curiously, raising his eyebrow. "You've *never* been to a beach before?"

Cher shakes her head, pouting her lips with shy embarrassment.

"Well if you stay here in L.A. with me, you can come every day- but not until it gets warmer. So come on out now."

Pharaoh quickly sweeps Cher up in his arms. Cher can tell

from the effortless way he carries her that he is very strong. He gently places her feet back down on the boardwalk. Pharaoh and Cher drift slowly, almost hesitantly, back to his car; talking and laughing the entire way.

Prince Pharaoh Charming opens the door for Princess Cher. Her bottom squishes in his leather seat when she lowers herself into the car. Pharaoh gives her a disapproving look, but extends a little grace and a slight smile appears on his face. Cher watches him circle around to the driver's seat. She can't help but feel that she has found *her* man– the one man made just for her. His Big Mama's warnings have all but dissipated and evaporated in the heat of Cher's balmy fantasies of him. Cher has seen how generous and genial Pharaoh is with those he loves– careful to show his appreciation, and determined to protect them. Cher could not fathom the man that Big Mama described and hoped that she would never be able to. She figures if she can gain Pharaoh's trust and be a security for him, something he's never had in a woman, then she will never know his wrath.

Cher has met many men with many vices, all of them trying ever so desperately to hide some dark underbelly, but none of them have ever come close to exhibiting the gentle goodness that she sees in Pharaoh. Cher contemplates his proposal. She still isn't sure what her decision will be in the morning. She does enjoy his company, but even still– she isn't sure if she is ready to abandon her whole life and commit to a new one with Pharaoh in LA. That is a lot of pressure to put on two and a half days. Cher decides to put it out of her mind. Either way the cards fall, she wants to spend the rest of this day enjoying Pharaoh's company in his City of Angels.

\*\*\*\*

The sun is just beginning to set when they arrive back at Pharaoh's pad. Cher races up to his apartment, eager to catch a glimpse of the view she missed yesterday. She holds her breath, as the last of the fiery orb descends into the water. The reflection of the sunrays in the sea glisten, making the sun look like a golden scoop of butter melting on a pancake. The sight of the sunset is so beautiful that Cher's eyes moisten with the expectation of tears that do not come. Instead, a bright smile appears on her face.

"I used to think that this view was the most beautiful thing that I would ever behold- until I first saw you," Pharaoh remarks lowly, kissing her hand. Cher blushes at the compliment.

"Cher," he starts with a sudden discomfort. "I have a previous engagement this evening, a very important gathering with my business associates."

"You mean like a shindig," Cher replies with a sly grin.

"Something like that– yes," Pharaoh admits shyly. "I generally do not cross my personal affairs with my business, but I do not want to spend what could be our last night together, apart from you." Pharaoh slips his arms around her waist and pulls her tightly to him. Cher breathes in his cologne, a bold yet understated musk. She lays her head against his firm chest and he rests his head on hers. "Would you like to accompany me to the event?" He asks cordially.

"I wish you had asked me earlier, so I could pick up some boss threads," Cher sighs with a deep frown.

"Actually, I hope you don't mind, but I took the liberty of

having my couturier design a dress just for you. This is my gift to you for coming here to be with me."

"Thank you," Cher squeaks with apprehension, trying desperately to feign gratitude. Cher is concerned that Pharaoh's fashion aesthetic may not compliment her style. "Are you sure it will fit?" Cher asks, hoping to find a diplomatic way out of having to wear the dress.

"I sent some of your clothes over with my request, so I should hope so." Pharaoh smiles, sensing Cher's hesitation. "Go get dressed, filet," he urges in a direct tone. "I'll see you in a short while." He kisses the tip of her nose.

Pharaoh brought two garment bags up from the car with him. Cher assumed that both were his, maybe some dry-cleaning. But as Pharaoh takes one of the bags and disappears up the staircase, she realizes that the other one belongs to her.

An hour later, they both emerge from their separate rooms. Pharaoh descends the staircase and convenes with Cher in the living room. Surprisingly, Cher beat him getting dressed. But not to be out done, she looks so stunning that Pharaoh applauds her as he crosses the room.

Cher must admit that Pharaoh has impeccable taste. He dons a silver sharkskin suit with a black dress shirt, buttoned down to expose the weight in silver that he wears around his neck. The cut of the suit is so infallible that it fits him like an expensive, well-tailored glove.

Likewise, Cher's dress is sophisticated and classy, yet still stylish and unique. Cher knew that she would be the only woman in the place to wear this fashion. She could imagine the dress on a European White woman walking the streets of Paris or Milan. The little black and white dress is made of soft, lustrous cashmere. Its long flowing sleeves are black on the outside and white on the inside. Her dress has a square neckline, which gathers under her bust before cascading down just above her knees in soft, layered black and white pleats. Pharaoh chose to complete her outfit with fancy, white-leather calf boots. Cher is so proud of Pharaoh for knowing just how to dress her.

"Beautiful." He beams, spreading her arms wide to inspect his work. He seems so impressed with himself at first, but then a look of concern spreads over his face. "Something is missing."

Pharaoh goes to his bedroom and returns with a flat, square, black velvet box. Cher covers her mouth with her hands before he even opens it. Her amazement grows when he reveals the contents. Inside lay a white diamond studded necklace and dangling, diamond snowflake earrings.

"This is too much," Cher breathes in astonishment.

Pharaoh holds up his right hand, displaying his authority like a policeman stopping traffic. Cher falls silent, letting her mouth remain still, even though she can feel the racing of her heart in the back of her throat. She holds her hair while Pharaoh fastens the necklace. Cher places the earrings into her lobes, then slowly turns to face him.

"There... Now that's perfect," he says finally, smoothing her hair.

"It sure is." Cher swoons, flashing a smile that gushes with her infatuation for him.

"Let's burn up the road, Mama."

**\*\*\*\***

The party is in Beverly Hills at the mansion of some

wealthy, Hollywood benefactor. Pharaoh breezes into the function with Cher on his right arm, while Benny and Blaze follow closely behind. All eyes in the room are on them when they stroll to the bar at the back of the parlor. The bartender abruptly stops what he is doing to take Pharaoh's request. Then, as if by sleight of hand, the bartender promptly places a wide-mouth glass before him. Pharaoh takes a small sip of the rum and coke, then lets his elbow come to rest on the counter, content to remain at the rear of the room. Cher swiftly realizes that Pharaoh is not anti-social, but strategic in his choices. She watches his eyes dart around the room. Pharaoh can watch the door and survey the entire scene from his vantage point at the bar.

The first level of the house is full of funky people in colorful get-ups. Cher glances around and observes that she and Pharaoh are in a class by themselves. The party is live by Cher's standards. She could definitely dig the groovy atmosphere. Females in multicolored mini-skirts with intricately-painted faces and long feathered eyelashes dance around handing out party favors. The music is disco with an upbeat tempo, just the way Cher likes it. "Do It" by B.T. Express blares throughout the house.

Cher taps her foot to the rhythm. With every fiber in her being, she wants to dance but decides against it, not knowing if Pharaoh will approve. Instead, she stays tight to his side, which proved to be a much better decision as the night went on. Cher could see that Pharaoh was quite popular by how many people drifted up to greet him.

"What's hap'nin'?", "Slide me some skin, Boss", "What it be like, Brother man?"

One by one, what seems like an endless stream of people approach Pharaoh at the bar, some even famous celebrities.

When Eddie Kendricks comes over to give a quiet salutation to Pharaoh, Cher is completely star-struck. Eddie is even more attractive in real life than he was on her television screen. She almost screams as he and Pharaoh whisper to each other, but she contains herself not wanting to appear immature in front of Pharaoh's business associates.

The stream continues on without interruption, as a tiny crowd forms around Pharaoh and Cher. Pharaoh is visited by the likes of Pam Grier, Pete Rose and a strange, keen-looking young White man named Steven Spielberg. Pharaoh whispers to a confused and uninterested Cher that Steven is an up and coming Hollywood movie director.

Still, Cher finds it amazing to see how influential Pharaoh is. The scene created by his presence at the party makes Cher wonder what kind of occupation he could have that would put him in contact with people from so many different races and walks of life. For whatever reason, people seem to respect him. Although Cher got a few subtle glances, Pharaoh never introduced her to anyone and none of his associates ever addressed her. Cher was beginning to think she got all dressed up for no reason at all. She had, yet again, become the invisible woman in the room.

Pharaoh maintains an aloof, mystifying presence. Benny and Blaze rove and patrol, but always remain within inches of him. By the expression on all of their faces, they are very obviously at work and not at all included in any festivities.

Pharaoh leans over to Cher, nudging her cheek with the tip of his nose as he speaks– offering just a small gesture of affection for her in public.

"I have a spot of business to take care of and then we can go wherever you want." Pharaoh gazes into her eyes intently, waiting for her nod of affirmation.

"Get Down Tonight" by K.C. and the Sunshine Band begins to trail off when a small, dark brown-skinned fox with a large, soft Afro slides her hand over Pharaoh's shoulder. His attention quickly turns away from Cher and to the buxom female. He seems appalled by the prospect of her touching him. Pharaoh's brows furrow and he casually brushes her hand away. His eyes search instantly for Benny and Blaze who are responsible for allowing an infiltration of his personal space.

"Hey, Boss," she squeaks in a sassy tone, chewing on her gum like a horse. She poses seductively with her hands on her hips. "You look banging tonight."

"Be still, woman. I don't appreciate you stepping to me like that." Pharaoh finally acknowledges Cher for the first time since they got there. "Don't you see my lady standing right here?"

"I see a lot of females standing around," the chick snaps back. "That don't mean a damn thing, Pharaoh. Ain't none of these broads got shit on me and you know it."

At that comment, Pharaoh dismisses her with a quick flip of his hand before reaching for his glass. Benny and Blaze who were watching the situation closely, awaiting an indication from Pharaoh of how to proceed, sweep in and escort the female away, pulling her by the elbow.

"I apologize," Pharaoh utters sincerely, with a slight tinge of embarrassment. "Just get whatever you want from the bar and I will be back in a few minutes, filet."

Cher nods and Pharaoh strides gracefully across the room.

He is met by two other Black men and one, possibly Italian, man. They all exchange a few quick words and then climb the stairs to the second level.

Cher orders a ginger ale from the bar and takes a few sips. With her newfound freedom, she begins to explore the room. She shuffles her feet just a little when "Lady Marmalade" comes blasting through the speakers. The boogie is contagious because many of the females begin to clap and chant like rowdy cheerleaders.

"Hey Sistah! Go Sistah! Soul Sistah! Go Sistah!"

Cher allows her head to bob a bit as she meanders through the crowd. She looks out of the large glass doors that open to the waterfall pool at the back of the house. People are spread out all over the lawn, conversing and smoking. Inside a few partygoers take turns, snorting long white lines off the mirror tables. Still overall, the scene is pretty subdued as far as parties go.

Before she knows it, Cher is lost in the music. She closes her eyes and involuntarily begins a slight gyration of her hips, accompanied by a few finger snaps.

"Mirage–" a husky-voiced stranger whispers in her ear. Cher spins around wildly, startled by the sudden interruption. "Whoa Mama, don't spill your drink," he says with a tiny laugh.

Cher makes sure to show the aggravation on her face while shaking ginger ale from her hand. She flips her long hair over her shoulder and starts to walk away without giving him any eye attention, but he grips her elbow tightly. Cher turns sharply to look at him– the offense apparent in her eyes. She doesn't recognize the light-skinned, hazel-eyed man. He looks vaguely

familiar with his thick lips and freckles, but still Cher can't
quite place him. She figures he has seen her dance since he used
her Thoroughbred name.

"Are you the entertainment at this shindig?...Cause I'd pay
anything to see you dance again." Cher would not have even
noticed it, although it was quite visible in the tight, white pants
he wore, until the stranger made it a point to get her attention by
grabbing his insignificant erection with unwarranted pride.
"You definitely the finest bitch between here and Vegas, but I
didn't know you took your little act on the road," he hisses
slyly; his voice as slimy as old motor oil. He leans in close to
Cher's ear. "If I knew that, I would have booked you for a
private gig at my crib-"

Before he can finish the sentence Cher slaps the words clean
out of his mouth. The pop of her hand against his face is so loud
that it hushes the room. Cher hit him so hard that he staggers
backward from the force. Cher's eyes blaze with rage that is
quickly matched by the man, once he regains his bearings. His
face turns bright red more from his anger and embarrassment
than Cher's assault.

In her fury, Cher finally recognizes him. He is one of the
men that was with Pharaoh the night she first saw him in Vegas.
The man advances aggressively towards Cher with clenched
fists. He moves forward undeterred, until Pharaoh's hand
appears on his shoulder. The man stops immediately, as though
Pharaoh's touch froze him in place. His anger dissipates quickly
when their eyes meet.

"What's the problem here, Leroy?" Pharaoh asks coolly with
clear, dark eyes. Pharaoh stands between him and Cher, who
was still huffing out angry breaths from the fierce rage that

wrestles within her. She breathes deeply, trying to calm herself before she explodes. Cher is sober-minded enough to know that she doesn't want Pharaoh to see her bug completely out.

Pharaoh wraps his hand gently around the back of Cher's neck, showing his possession of her. His touch does the trick, quelling the savage beast. Like a salve, his hand calms her temper and quenches the fire. The anger shifts like transference from Cher to Pharaoh, as he stares with hostility at Leroy, patiently awaiting his answer.

Then almost as if on cue, "Fire" by the Ohio Players pipes into the room. The music continues to play on even though everyone in the room is still and silent, watching the scene develop between Pharaoh and Leroy.

"Nothing's wrong, Pharaoh. We a'ight." Leroy's answer is more of an appeal, like a petition to Pharaoh, than a statement. "Everything is fine here."

"Cher," Pharaoh says quietly, turning his eyes to her. "Is everything okay here?"

"Hell no, it's not okay. That jive turkey disrespected me."

Benny and Blaze move in instantly from behind Leroy, but before they touch him, Pharaoh holds up his hand.

"I'll handle this," Pharaoh states diplomatically. Both men stop short and cross their arms across their chest, as if on standby.

"Leroy, to disrespect my lady is to disrespect me."

"I would never disrespect you Pharaoh," Leroy pleads. "I swear I didn't know she was yours."

Even in the heat of the exchange, something about the way Leroy said *yours* turns Cher on. Cher could see that her man was **The Man** in the place and she felt privileged to have him champion her. Being on his arm, made Cher feel like the luckiest woman in the world.

"Leroy–" Pharaoh begins philosophically. "If you see a hundred dollar bill sitting on a counter, it's not okay to touch it just because the owner is not there. This ain't grade school. Ain't no finders keepers up in here. We're too grown for that. To touch what does not belong to you is very dangerous. Didn't your mother teach you anything?" Pharaoh asks presenting his palm to Leroy. "I have seen men killed for less than what you have done." The seriousness of Pharaoh's threat is displayed in his cold stare.

"Look Pharaoh," Leroy stutters, licking his lips. "I apologize for disrespecting your lady. I wouldn't have done that if I knew she was with you."

"That's my problem with you Leroy. You obviously need to learn some manners... a little home training, cause a man should never approach a female that way, regardless of who she's with." Pharaoh takes his hand from Cher's neck and steps closer to Leroy. "If you had given my woman the opportunity, she would have told you who her Daddy is, then you wouldn't be caught up in all this confusion right now." Pharaoh rolls his shoulders forward and glares at Leroy with contempt.

"I understand Pharaoh and it won't happen again," Leroy utters solemnly, his chin quivering ever so slightly.

"Well I'm glad you do… but so that you don't forget–" Pharaoh grabs Leroy in a move so swift and seamless that you could have missed it if you blinked. The only evidence that Pharaoh touched him at all was the sound of a cracking pop followed by Leroy's howling shrieks.

"Benny, take care of Leroy, please."

Leroy clutches his left arm so tightly that Cher couldn't assess the damage Pharaoh did to him. Benny drags him, screaming and crying the entire way.

Cher felt good but at the same time guilty that Pharaoh had to stand up for her. She was upset that she caused him to make a scene in front of his business associates. Although the attendants were back to party as usual just as soon as Leroy was gone, Cher still couldn't help but feel that it would not have happened if she hadn't been there. On the other hand, seeing Pharaoh handle Leroy, who was twice his build, with such swift precision made her panties wet.

Pharaoh takes Cher by the hand and leads her through the glass doors, out to the patio behind the house. They walk out on the grounds to a quiet, secluded space by the tall hedges. Cher silently hopes that Pharaoh is not upset with her. She only wants him to be satisfied with her. She remains quiet as they walk, allowing him a clear opportunity to speak if he wishes to. Cher is taken by surprise when he says–

"Isn't this such a beautiful night?" Pharaoh poses the question playfully, as if none of the previous events just happened.

"You're not upset with me, are you?" Cher bites her lip, ashamed of the circumstances.

"No. Why should I be?" Pharaoh smiles at her. "You looked like you had it under control."

Cher can't help but smile as well. "I just don't want to cause any problems for you in your business. I know you didn't want to bring me here tonight and now look what happened." Cher is so frustrated that she throws up her hands in defeat but Pharaoh won't have it. He rubs her shoulder to console her.

"That incident had nothing to do with my business and it had nothing to do with you. That was about respect– my respect. Nothing more. I didn't hurt Leroy bad, he'll be fine. A bone will mend in time, but my reputation cannot be so easily repaired. Anyone that I associate with is a reflection of who I am as a man. My men and I are very well-respected in this community, so I cannot have anyone thinking that I would condone or even tolerate behavior like Leroy's in my organization. But again, you don't need to worry about any of that." Pharaoh gently brushes her cheek with the back of his hand. "Pharaoh will never allow another man to touch what is his."

His eyes burn with a consuming passion that draws Cher into its flames. Her body yearns for him. She feels herself responding to the invisible touch of his intense stare.

"The only thing Cher has to do is to decide... whether she wants to be mine– all and only mine... or not."

"Pharaoh, I-"

"No," he interrupts, pressing his finger to her lips. "Not yet."

The melody of "Show and Tell" by Al Wilson drifts out across the grounds to them. Cher leans demurely against Pharaoh. Looking up into his eyes lovingly, she lets him know that she wants to express the intimacy of the moment with him. Pharaoh casually obliges and pulls her closer to him. She lays her head against his chest. He takes her hands and rests them on his shoulders before encircling his arms around her waist. He sways slightly and Cher responsively follows his lead. Cher can tell, even from the modest slow drag, that Pharaoh is a good dancer. Cher doesn't care. His body feels so good pressed against hers.

The dance just feels... *right*.

Cher can feel Pharaoh's love for her... right there– in the dance... and she smiles at the thought of it.

"Let me get you home," Pharaoh sighs quietly into her ear. He takes her hand and leads her back to the house. Blaze is waiting by the glass doors for them. Pharaoh instructs him to bring the car around.

They make the ride back to Pharaoh's crib in almost total silence. Pharaoh stares out of the window the whole time, seemingly lost in deep, meaningful meditation. When they return to the apartment, Pharaoh gives Cher a light kiss on the cheek and heads upstairs. After being shot down the night before, Cher didn't bother to follow him or otherwise solicit any more affection from him. She knew better than to appear to be a glutton for punishment.

Still, she couldn't believe that the night ended so benignly, but she is glad for the solitude. It will give her time to clear her head, arrange her thoughts, recap the events of the day and hopefully be prepared to make an informed decision in the morning.

Cher slinks through Pharaoh's bedroom door and into the bathroom. She undresses and then jumps into a scalding shower. She scrubs her skin, trying to wash away all that unnerves her; all the apprehension, the fears, the anxieties. She hopes that they will just roll away, down the drain with the water. But she soon realizes, when she twists the knob and her feet touch the cold, tile floor, that those emotions are (at least for the time being) a permanent fixture in her head.

Cher drops down into Pharaoh's bed, too exhausted to even slip into one of his shirts as she usually does. Although this is her third night in his bed, it is her first time feeling his satin sheets against her bare skin. The smooth fabric tickles her nipples and caresses her hips. Cher feels an erotic intoxication as she imagines that the soft satin is Pharaoh's hands on her naked flesh. Eventually her arousal dissipates long enough for her to fall off into a light sleep...

\*\*\*\*

Cher is sure she's dreaming when she stirs suddenly. Dreaming is something she has done a lot of since she came to California. She feels the warmth of his body against hers, seeping into her sleep. It is his hands that finally wake her; his roving hands exploring her body and shattering her slumber. Even when Cher opens her eyes and sees Pharaoh over her, she still holds on firmly to the notion that she is in a vivid dream.

When he kisses her neck, she begins to recognize that this is a dream, but it's her dream finally come true. Pharaoh lays behind her, rubbing his large hands over her rotund breasts, stroking and caressing them. His hands slide down her stomach and over her thick, shapely thighs. Cher sighs heavily. Her body weakens as she releases her inhibitions to him. He lifts her knee and brushes his hand along the inside of her thighs. His fingers find her flower. He parts the petals and gently massages her clitoris.

Cher blooms for him. "Oh Pharaoh," she coos, when he plunges his fingers deep inside of her. They both moan together from the sheer ecstasy of the small pleasure. The feeling of Cher's tight flesh and warm syrup on his fingers makes Pharaoh's organ thump, so engorged with blood that it is almost painful for him. His erect manhood presses firmly against her round, voluptuous buttocks. Pharaoh grips her hips tightly, longing so desperately to push his throbbing serpent inside the moistness of her femininity.

Cher yearns to feel his love inside of her too. She can feel Pharaoh rubbing his organ between her butt cheeks, but he refuses to enter her. Cher reaches back to caress his manhood and possibly encourage his penetration. She realizes when her hand slips around his long, thick penis that it is bigger in her hand than it had appeared in his shorts.

Cher instantly becomes nervous and insecure. She has only been with two other men, if you count the Reverend, and neither of them had anything comparable to what is in her hand now. Fears and insecurities, the likes of which Cher never considered when she was dreaming of this moment, flood her mind. She begins to wonder if she can please Pharaoh. Cher can tell by the way he licks along her spine, sending delightful chills throughout her body, that he is skillful. Pharaoh, being the intuitive lover that he is, senses the tension and stops his seduction.

"What's wrong, Cher?" He asks, stroking her hair away from her face.

"Nothing Papa." Cher lies, but cannot convince him. Pharaoh can feel the stress that has seeped into her muscles. Pharaoh rolls Cher onto her back, separates her thighs and then climbs between them. She feels his manhood on her femininity, but Pharaoh doesn't make any attempt to penetrate her. He just relaxes against her stomach, gently brushing his fingers across her forehead.

"Talk to me, Love. I can't trust you if you refuse to be open and honest with me." He kisses her lips tenderly and nudges the tip of his nose against hers.

Cher feels so embarrassed. She doesn't want to admit that

she is afraid of his love. She knows that Pharaoh has had many women before her and doesn't want to pale in comparison. She doesn't want to disappoint him.

"I couldn't wait until the morning," Pharaoh continues, negating his previous petition. Cher is glad that he didn't push the issue and require an answer of her. She just listens attentively to his words instead. "I want to know now. I *need* to know. I can't even sleep, that's how bad you got me spinning, baby." Pharaoh kisses her again deeply, letting his tongue caress hers. Cher becomes lightheaded with passion and her lips tingle as he sucks on each one.

"I have to know. Are you mine? ... Will you stay with me?"

Cher answers yes, before he can ask the question. She sighs her affirmations on such low, soft breaths that Pharaoh misses them the first time.

"Yes?" he asks, ensuring that he hears her correctly.

"Yes," Cher confirms with nods.

Pharaoh smiles slowly, a smile that doesn't stop where it should. His smile is so huge, it threatens to need its own zip code. He hugs her tightly to him, kissing her neck.

"Are you *absolutely*... **positively** sure?" Pharaoh stresses, staring directly into her eyes.

"Yes," Cher puffs with facetious irritation. She rolls over on top of him and kisses along his chest. Pharaoh drops his head back onto the pillows, enjoying the momentary pleasure of her lips on his body. He runs his fingers through her soft hair that drapes across his stomach. Then suddenly, he rolls her back underneath him.

"No, Mama," Pharaoh asserts, reclaiming control. He pins her hands down on the bed. "Tonight, it's all about you."

Pharaoh begins to suck on her nipples, those vulnerable nipples that have begged daily for his mouth. A moan escapes Cher's lips. She can feel her love begin to come down as her nectar drips onto the bed. Cher can't believe that the feeling of his strong lips, tugging on her tender, erect nipples is enough to compel her climax, but it is. Her walls throb with anticipation. Pharaoh kisses a trail down her stomach to the thin layer of curly fuzz on her peach.

Pharaoh spreads her thighs apart. Cher is confused by his head being so close to her chocha. She doesn't really know why he's down there. She just figures that he is inspecting her goods… until he tastes her.

Cher had never known the pleasure of a man's tongue on her love. A shockwave of such unbelievable bliss rips through her body that she cannot contain it. Cher's hips buck against Pharaoh's face before she can suppress the urge. He watches her excitement with his dark, alluring eyes. Pharaoh is genuinely surprised, but enticed by the gratification that Cher is receiving from him. He sucks long and hard, then licks her petals anxiously like an ice cream cone that will melt if he doesn't. His long, thick tongue feels so wonderful to her that Cher cannot catch her breath.

She moans uncontrollably, "Oh, god... mmm, Oh, god." writhing and thrashing on the bed while he presses his tongue deeper and deeper inside of her. Cher's back arches and her toes curl, as she balls up tight fistfuls of bedding.

Pharaoh rubs his thumb across her clit and delves two long, soft fingers inside of her tight hole. He quickly finds Cher's G-spot and flicks it as though it is a climax light switch. Pharaoh lightly kisses her petals with his warm, silky lips, then rolls his tongue quickly; purring like an engine and creating a vibrating sensation.

Cher goes wild. Her body whips forward in the bed, as Pharaoh finishes her off. His face is buried so deep between her thighs that she clutches his head for balance. He holds her thighs apart to keep from suffocating while she melts into his mouth. Cher howls so loud with her orgasm, that it sounds like a painful cry– but pain is not what Cher is feeling–

Cher is feeling a rapture so beautiful, it makes her delirious. She bites down hard on her lip to distract from the overwhelming ecstasy. As her climax ebbs, Cher collapses heavy against the bed– out of breath, gasping for air, like she just ran a marathon. Her body is burning up on the inside; but on the outside, her skin is cool with sweat. She tingles from head to cramped toe as goose bumps appear.

"Oh god, Pharaoh." Cher groans, with her hand on her forehead.

"You don't have to worship me." Pharaoh smiles, wiping his lips and moustache. "I already know that I am god."

Pharaoh pulls on his boxer briefs, then pats Cher's thigh, as he stands up from the bed. Cher thought he was going into the bathroom to clean up, but instead he heads for the bedroom door.

"Where are you going?" Cher asks anxiously.

"I'm going back to bed," Pharaoh replies simply.

"But aren't we going to... you know?" Cher feels the embarrassment again. She is still very nervous about experiencing his love.

"I think you've had enough for one night," Pharaoh says

playfully. "I know your mouth and your heart said yes tonight, but I still don't have your mind. Until I have that, there's a part of you that's not mine." Pharaoh runs his hands over his toned stomach. "You can't have all of me until I have all of you."

The truth and gravity of what Pharaoh just said weighs suddenly on Cher's heart like an anvil. He is right. She doesn't trust him completely. Pharaoh definitely isn't a selfish lover, so Cher could understand his reservations. Cher is not used to a man being so in control of his will that he can resist her sexually, but Cher could tell that Pharaoh cares deeply for her and his refusal to bed her shows that he can be trusted with her heart. Cher is grateful to him for what he gave, but also for what he withheld.

"Goodnight, Cher," Pharaoh whispers, slipping from the bedroom.

****

Cher awoke early the next morning, still surprisingly exhausted from her encounter with Pharaoh. Since Cher would be a permanent fixture in his crib, she wanted to pull her weight and show her worth by catering to Pharaoh, beginning with breakfast on their first official morning as an item.

The dismay shows on Cher's face when she enters the kitchen to find Pharaoh is already there, with a spatula in hand, turning over pancakes in a skillet. Her unexpected presence slightly startles him.

"Good morning, Love. You're up early." He scoops the pancake from the pan, quickly placing it atop a stack on the plate. He turns the stove off and swoops Cher into his arms.

"Mmm," he moans low and long, kissing Cher so passionately that her knees buckle. Pharaoh's strong arms support her weight and he crushes her against his chest. Cher is so elated. She can already tell the difference in Pharaoh now that she is his woman. A little more of his wall comes down, revealing even more of this beautiful man for her to discover.

"I'm a man of my word. It's the morning. Are you sure you still want to stay?"

Cher presses her palms against Pharaoh's chest and rolls her eyes. "How many times do I have to tell you, Papa. Yes... yes... and yes. I'm here to stay and I'm all yours."

Pharaoh's head drops back and he lets out a hearty, jovial laugh, as he lifts Cher up off of the floor. She hugs his neck tightly; their lips locking into a deep kiss. Cher hopes the interlude will progress back to the bedroom, a continuation of the session that began last night, but Pharaoh lowers her back to her feet and says instead–

"I gotta' get going. I have a few errands to run before my meetings."

Cher groans. "It's Saturday. Do you have meetings *every* day?"

"Yes," Pharaoh answers plainly. "Just about every day." Cher frowns deeply and takes her plate to the table.

"Look, Cher. I care about you. I will make as much time as I can to spend with you, but my business requires constant supervision. When the Boss is away, the mice will play. Everyone who saw you with me at that party knows that for the first time in a very long time, I am tied down. They'll be waiting for me to start slipping and laying down on the job, so they can edge me out of the competition."

"I don't know any businessman who works on the weekend. Just what exactly is it that you do anyway?" Cher asks boldly, so sassy in fact, that she shocks herself with the assertion of her tone. Cher observes the change in Pharaoh's expression. He glares at her like a disapproving patriarch. She gets the hint and tries to smooth over her offense. "I just want to be with you, Papa. That's all." She retracts shyly. "Can't we have a little honeymoon time?" Cher bats her eyes.

Pharaoh can't help but smile at her. She is so alluring to him. She knows just how to use what she has to disarm him: her lashes, her smile... her thighs. Her eyes capture him and for just a moment he believes her. He pushes his reservations aside and just enjoys her seduction.

"I don't have much to do today, so we can spend time together this afternoon. I can take you shopping before we go out to dinner."

"You know I *can* cook. I'm not half-bad either. I would like the chance to show you, sometime."

"You can feel free to do whatever you want to around here, Mama. This is your home now. I just want to pamper you. Let me know if I'm overbearing in my attempts to take care of you."

"I appreciate everything you do for me," Cher replies, hugging his waist tightly. "I just want to take as good care of you, as you do of me."

"Okay, make a grocery list of what you need and have it delivered. I will help you with dinner, when I come back." Pharaoh pecks her cheek. "Go ahead and eat your breakfast before it gets cold."

"What about you?" Cher asks curiously.

"I've already had breakfast."

"Well tomorrow, for a change, I'm making you breakfast.

What do you say to some French crepes?"

"Sounds great, but you'll have to get up way early to fix breakfast for me."

Cher ponders the predicament. "When do you get up in the morning?"

"Long before you do," Pharaoh replies sarcastically.

"Okay, well I'll just set an alarm. I'll be up when you come down tomorrow."

"Absolutely not. No alarm clocks in my pad. I don't want the peaceful sanctity of my morning interrupted by loud noises. Besides, it wouldn't make a difference. You'll never beat me to the kitchen. Not even the sun beats me waking up in the morning." Pharaoh issues his arrogant dare.

"You wait and see. Pharaoh is getting a breakfast cooked by his woman tomorrow. Just watch!" Cher retorts brazenly, accepting the challenge.

"Alright, Mama." Pharaoh flashes Cher an irresistible smile. "We'll see."

****

The day passed most uneventfully. Cher watched television on the sofa in her Wonder Woman T-shirt and red mini shorts. She ordered lunch and caught an episode of her favorite television program, "Good Times".

Pharaoh's meetings ran long, so he didn't return to the crib until after eight. He entreated Cher's forgiveness, promising that the entire Sunday would be hers and (in a gesture of good faith) took her out for dinner. When Cher was asked what kind of food she was in the mood for, she answered Chinese. Pharaoh, dependable as ever, delivered with a beautifully traditional restaurant in New Chinatown which served delectable Asian cuisine.

"Goodnight, Cher." Pharaoh issues his usual night salutation and kisses her cheek, before ascending the stairs to the upper level.

Cher tossed in his bed that night. She laid there with one eye open, partially hoping that Pharaoh would join her again, as he had the night before. Cher had finally come to accept his principles and his restraint, but still she wanted to feel the warmth of his body spooning with her at night. Eventually her restlessness drove her out of the bed to the living room. Cher was convinced that it would be best to doze there, then she would be sure to beat Pharaoh out for breakfast because he would have to pass her on his way to the kitchen.

Cher blinked heavily, wrapping herself in a blanket before settling down on the sofa. She snoozed lightly for a few hours, sitting straight up with her head leaning against her palm. Cher woke every few minutes, when her head would roll off her hand. A small price to pay, in her mind, for catering to her man.

Hours before dawn, according to the sun clock above Pharaoh's television– at 5:11 am, a faint rustling sound wakes Cher. She listens to Pharaoh move around above the living room. She waits a few minutes for him to come down. She doesn't want to begin breakfast too early and then it be cold, so she waits.

Fifteen minutes later, the shuffling noises continue, but Pharaoh never appears on the stairs. Soon, the curiosity drives Cher out on a discovery mission. She mounts the steps and goes just far enough up the staircase for her eyes to be level with the floor. She looks through the railings into the room on the right.

## Pharaoh Forever

All she can see is Pharaoh's profile. He eyes are closed and he is kneeling on the padded floor in a black, karate gi uniform. His head is lowered and his hands rest on top of his thighs. He breathes deeply, as Cher watches him.

"Come here, sweetheart," he whispers softly with his eyes closed. Cher, still wrapped in her blanket, takes the last few steps and moves in a quick, Geisha-like shuffle towards the room. She stops at the doorway.

"Right here, Love." He pats a spot on the floor to the right of him.

Cher sits Indian-style and they remain quiet for some time. Cher studies the bare room. It has a serene, heavenly quality, completely white from the padded floor to the ceiling, save one mirror wall. The room, with its adjoining bathroom and closet, was most likely originally designed to be a second bedroom; but obviously, Pharaoh converted it for the purpose of being his personal dojo space. A hideaway bed is tucked into the wall, so Cher discerns that this is where Pharaoh sleeps. Cher feels blessed to be invited into the sanctity of his morning meditation session. Her meager sacrifice of a few-hours sleep wasn't worthy to be compared with this reward. This time with Pharaoh helps her to better understand his restraint, his energy, and his spirit.

Cher comprehends, sitting there beside him, that the source of his power and authority begins in this space with him first mastering his own will. She is more impressed with him than ever. Pharaoh turns his palms over on his thighs, facing them up towards the ceiling.

"Cher, do you know why I always keep you at my right hand?"

Cher glances in the mirror to see that she is indeed at his right side and recalls, when she thinks back over the days, that is her usual place.

"When two people share the same position– that is to say the same dominion, there has to be an order. There has to be organization or chaos will ensue."

Cher remains silently attentive, allowing Pharaoh to philosophize and expound on his disciplines.

"Although the authority of the office is shared by both, whichever entity is enthroned on the left is greater in power than that which is on the right, but this is only to preserve the order."

Cher listens intently, trying not to allow her confusion to show. Pharaoh's precepts are a little over her head, but she throws her reason and logic out of the window and just relishes the experience of his smooth baritone voice.

"Cher, I have invited you to share my reign with me. You have the same authority that I have over whatever is mine. At your word, goddess, whatever request or desire you have will be accomplished. You alone have the power and strength of my heart to will even me to obey your command." Pharaoh opens his eyes; dark and focused, they remain steady on her. His gaze is so intimidating that she lowers her eyes from his face to the floor. "With a power that magnificent, there comes great responsibility. I, Pharaoh, remain Supreme, but all that I am– my life, is yours to share with me, so long as you understand that my word is the only law."

Something about his final message unnerves her, but she is far too focused on his admission that she has his heart to pay the warning its due attention.

"Forget all that you believe in, all that you subscribe to. There should be no other thought or belief more sovereign in your mind than my words."

Cher doesn't know what the word *sovereign* means, so she just nods slowly.

"When you have yielded that place to me and trust me completely to command your life the way I trust you with mine, then– and only then, can we become one."

A chill travels down Cher's spine at the prospect of that. She knows that she is supposed to be soaking up all of this heavy knowledge, but Cher can't help being distracted by his supple lips. The thought of them on her chocha causes her blood to boil and she cannot concentrate.

Pharaoh stands to his feet and helps Cher to hers. She wasn't sure what Pharaoh's whole monologue was about, but she knows that she feels safe with him and secure in the love that is developing in her.

"Thank you for joining me this morning," Pharaoh says diplomatically.

"It was my pleasure," Cher answers courteously. "I'm glad for the opportunity to participate. I never thought that such a peaceful room lay behind this door. I was secretly afraid that an arsenal of guns or drugs were stored in here," Cher admits honestly.

"Oh no. **Never**. I do not handle guns anymore. I relinquished even the notion of that when I ended my military career– and as for drugs, they are an obstruction to enlightenment. You will never catch me with them in my temple or in my home."

Cher is somewhat perplexed by Pharaoh's statement. She had never allowed her thoughts the free license to wander to the dark corners of her fears; but deep in the back of her mind, Cher figured that Pharaoh was a drug King Pin. How else could you explain his *business*? Still, she is relieved to hear him say that his crib is free from illegal activities.

"I have found that the most potent weapons, more destructive than guns or bombs, are the heart, the mind and also the hands, if used by someone who does not have mastery over the first two. A weapon is only dangerous in the hands of someone who intends to use it." Pharaoh studies his own hands, as he turns them over. "The mind and the heart are the source of all evil and all violence– every destructive force. That is why I need to know that you trust me with all of your heart and mind. If there is any doubt or suspicion within you towards me and my authority over you, then our love will never survive."

Pharaoh steps over to Cher and drapes his arms around her neck. He draws her tightly to his chest and rests his cheek on her head. "If you were concerned about this room or anything else in my home, you should have come to me. There is nothing in my life that I would hide from you. You are the queen in this kingdom and therefore privileged to even my most intimate meditation, should you desire to know it."

Cher felt herself melting into him. His words were finding their way into her heart, conquering all of her resistance. The last fortified battlements began to crumble under the force of his eloquent speech.

"Promise me, from now on, you will be transparent with me." Pharaoh rubs her cheek and finds there are tears on his fingers. "You alright, Mama." He steps back, looking into her eyes with sympathy.

"Yeah." She sighs long with tears rolling from her eyes. Pharaoh's expression turns to concern, as he studies her. "It's just so overwhelming sometimes."

"You mean- the move. I know this is difficult for you."

"No." Cher shakes her head. "Your love– It's hard for me to accept. It feels like too much."

"Well," Pharaoh smiles. "It may be more than you can handle but it's all yours. Do you want me to hold back and give it to you slowly, so you don't feel so much pressure on you?"

"No, I can take it." Cher grins through her tears. "It just takes *a lot* of getting used to."

"Well, practice makes perfect, baby." Pharaoh wraps one arm around her shoulders. "Because my love is not going anywhere."

Pharaoh takes off his uniform and hangs it in the closet, before slipping into brown cotton lounge pants. "The day is yours to will, Cher. What do you want to do?"

"Since I'm usually still asleep at this time, on any given day, what would Pharaoh do next?"

"Next, in my usual routine, is a shower and some coffee, then making breakfast for you."

"Okay well, I'm on it," Cher says confidently. "I told you that I would cook you breakfast today and I'm keeping my word."

"I have to give it to you. It's yo' thang, Mama. I'm impressed. You won the challenge."

Cher gloats, wagging her head side to side and sticking her tongue out at him. "Well I'll get started on my specialty," Cher says, shuffling out of the room. Pharaoh catches her blanket tail under his foot.

"May I interject?" Pharaoh asks politely.
Cher nods.

"If it pleases her majesty, I would not like to deviate from my morning routine."

"What do you mean? I can fix breakfast while you do whatever you like."

"Well, my shower is next and it would be out of sight, if you joined me." Pharaoh offers a slow, sly smile.

The shower proved to be an awesome start to their day together. The warm water spills over them like summer rain, softening their skin to the touch. Pharaoh's nude body, covered in droplets of rolling water, entices Cher's sensual appetite. Her skin is hypersensitive with arousal. The beads of water race down her breasts, tickling her nipples. As a few drops travel down, they find their way into her petals, stimulating her love and igniting her desire.

Pharaoh is more reserved than Cher expected. He lathers her back most expeditiously. He didn't even seem too interested in fooling around until it was Cher's turn to lather him. She gently washes his back, letting her hands rub over his sculpted shoulders, then down to the top of his firm buttocks. Cher slides her soapy hands around his waist, to the thick mass of soft hair and finds his manhood. It responds, flexing under her touch. It grows long and heavy in her hands when she caresses it. Pharaoh moans lowly, and drops his head back. He places his hands around hers and applies more pressure, length and vigor to her stroke. Cher becomes so aroused as her hands rub over the thick, throbbing veins. She even begins to relax at the notion of him entering her. After all, Pharaoh had many women before and it's not like his love killed any of them... right?

*What's the worst that could happen?*

Cher becomes increasingly sure, as she caresses his manhood that his love will be an extraordinary experience... magnificent, even. Cher can feel Pharaoh's body begin to tense. She is so delighted by his elation. Cher presses her breasts against his back, receiving an osmotic transfer of his ecstasy. Cher feels the intense pulsing in his organ and anxiously awaits his offering, but before Pharaoh can release his passion, he spins around in the shower and presses her body forcefully against the back wall. She feels him poking against her stomach, as he licks and sucks on her neck. Cher's arms drop to her sides as she surrenders to him. He lifts her up, hoisting her thighs around his narrow waist. Cher can feel his rigid manhood knocking on her door, pressing at the tender entrance of her love. Her femininity throbs, dripping with juicy anticipation, to receive him.

Suddenly, Pharaoh leans Cher back against the shower wall and lets her legs slide down. He reaches over and turns off the water, before handing her a towel.

"What's wrong?" Cher asks, confused and puzzled by how quickly Pharaoh's passion is extinguished. Within seconds his organ is little more than a flaccid piece of meat.

"Nothing," he offers dismissively, wrapping a towel around his waist. Pharaoh steps out of the tub and crosses the bathroom, to the mirror. He seems somewhat disturbed by the fact that he wet his hair in the shower, but brushes it vigorously to put it back into its sculpted place. Cher felt like a cold wet fish, hooked up and reeled in, then left out to die. Her lips tighten, as she angrily folds herself up in the towel. Pharaoh watches

Cher's expression in the mirror when she stomps out of the shower.

"Speak," he commands softly. Cher scowls at him, squinting her eyes. Pharaoh turns to face her. "Speak," he says, more directly this time, crossing his arms over his chest.

"What's the skinny, man? I'm getting a little fed up of all this jive you pulling, Pharaoh."
A faint grin of amusement appears on his face.

"I've accepted the fact that you don't want to go to bed with me. I have respected your principles, but you keep leading me on and then leaving me hanging. It just ain't copasetic. I'm starting to think that there's more to this abstinence than what you're telling me."

"If it's not for the reasons that I told you, then you tell me what it is?" Pharaoh raises an eyebrow.

"Are you a homosexual?"

Pharaoh's eyes widen. He shakes his head, then turns his back on Cher.

"So you're suspicious of my motives? You don't trust me, Cher?" He asks, spraying shaving foam into his hands.

Cher shuts down. She realizes she was being tested and just failed.

"No, Pharaoh. I didn't say that. I just don't feel desired when you treat me this way."

"You know," Pharaoh begins, swishing his razor under the running water. "That's just how I feel too. See how you instantly retreat back to your innocent act- like you're so into me. The truth is that you believe very dark and ugly things about me. This is the first thing to come out of your mouth when I don't respond how you want me to– or how you think I should... Are you playing with me, Cher?" Pharaoh asks, staring into her eyes through the mirror. His expression is serious and solemn.

"No Pharaoh. I truly care about you."

"So why is that true when you say it, but not when I do? Is it because you will have sex with me? Does that make your love more legitimate than mine?"

Cher feels like a mouse caught in a trap. She feels so guilty. She can see that Pharaoh is right. She isn't ready to love him.

"Well does it? Is it sex that validates love or is it the other way around. Because obviously, I must have it backwards. There must be something wrong with me because I don't want to be more physically involved with a woman than I am emotionally and spiritually involved with her. I guess if being homosexual means wanting to be in love before you commune in the flesh, then I must be some kind of sexual deviant. I suppose I should want to bed you, since you *obviously* have so much faith in me, Cher– since you *obviously* care so much about me, right?" Pharaoh finds his sarcasm so entertaining that he laughs lightly while cleaning his razor. "Has sex ever brought you true love, Cher?"

Cher is so ashamed of herself. She drops her head, tucking her chin against her chest and shakes her head.

"Isn't that strange?" He says in a surprised tone. "Maybe we have more in common than you think. Maybe you are homosexual too." He sucks his teeth. "'Cause I ain't never found true love in some pussy either."

Pharaoh keeps his tone so lighthearted that Cher doesn't realize how angry he really is.

"I'm sorry-"

"Don't apologize for how you feel. *I'm* obviously the Big, Bad Wolf for not sticking my dick in you, and *you're* the helpless victim. *I'm* the one who's playing a game with your emotions that I am evidently winning by *not* having sex with you. That is how you see it, right?"

"No, I don't think-"

"You know what I find to be the most bogus part of this whole situation?" Pharaoh pauses for her answer.

"Pharaoh, I didn't mean to-"

"I told you that you have my heart. I told you that I would accomplish your desires. I told you to give me the word and you can have from me whatever you want. If you wanted me to make love to you, if you wanted the responsibility that comes along with that privilege, then all you had to do was ask me." He stares at her intently. "You never once *asked* me to make love to you. My body was in your hands to will it, but you chose not to, then blamed me for not violating you."

Pharaoh begins to dress. He shoves his legs into his pants and Cher can tell that his temper is escalating. "You're silly and immature, Cher. You don't listen to me and worse– you don't learn from me."

Cher feels her heart breaking and she begins to cry. Pharaoh disregards her.

"Get out of my crib. I'll have Musah take you back to Vegas."

He leaves the bedroom quickly and barges out of the front door.

****

It was four long hours, possibly the longest hours of Cher's life before Pharaoh came back... She sat like a condemned woman, waiting for his return like an execution... But come back he did... and he came back to find Cher waiting for him in abject silence.

"Why are you still here?" he asks lowly; not angry, not pleasant. "I thought I told you to burn the road up."

"I couldn't leave," Cher says casually. Pharaoh, for the first time, looks perplexed by her. Cher appears sad and dejected, but there is a hopefulness in her tone.

"I couldn't go–" she repeats. "because I have the key." She smiles at him. "I have to keep it and I can't lose it, because it's the only one."

She steps over to him. "I have to be here to let you in when you come home." A large tear sits suspended on the rim of her left eye, as she holds up the small, silver key. "I finally get it Pharaoh. This key belongs to your heart and not just the apartment, doesn't it?"

He nods and bites down on his lip to fight back a smile.

"See, I can learn from you," she pleads. "Teach me how to love without fear."

"Quoi que tu souhaites," he whispers, taking her head into his hands. He kisses her deeply. Cher closes her eyes and the tear falls on their lips, seasoning the bittersweet kiss.

Pharaoh slept in his bed with Cher that night... because she asked him to. For the first time, she didn't long to be bedded by him. She was just thankful for the warm comfort of his presence. That was sufficient to satisfy her. Cher did not want to ask for his love that night and not be able to offer her soul in exchange. She wanted him to have her complete being. She realized that was what he was after. Cher didn't want to be selfish with Pharaoh and cheat him out of a deeper intimacy with her just because she wanted a physical thrill that would only be as momentary as the emotions which inspired it.

She laid that night, snuggled against his chest, listening to his heart beat long after he had fallen asleep. She was in love. She was sure of it. She wanted to take it slow, not because she had doubts, but because she wanted to prove to Pharaoh that she deserved him. She knew that he lost confidence in her and she wanted their love to be complete and unwavering when they finally lay down together.

In the darkness, she kisses his chest. Pharaoh, deep in sleep but disturbed by the gesture, rolls over on his side. Cher places her cheek against his back, just between his shoulder blades and slides her arm under his. Pharaoh stirs, and feeling her hand on him, he wraps his hand around hers and holds it against his chest, then drifts back off to sleep. Cher allows the cadence of his heartbeat to soothe her, as she leaves him there in the bed. She loses consciousness and finds her way back to him again... in a dream– a dream of Pharaoh holding her tightly in his arms. He embraces her and rocks her off to sleep, like a baby... just like a little baby.

*Shhh... Cher sleeps now*

# THE BODY ELECTRIC

Pharaoh proved to be just as dependable as an alarm clock.

Every morning he was up at 5am. Cher fell into the routine of preparing his breakfast at 6am, after Pharaoh finished his martial arts practice and showered. Each morning without fail, they would sit across the table from each other and chew in silence. All that's not to say that the beginning of their life together was mundane. The silence that lingered around them in the morning was an understanding, an intimacy; a sensual energy that smoldered in the quiet, as they stared over the plates and into each other eyes. Cher knew that nothing in their bodies, in their touch could compare to this connection. Pharaoh was in her head, in her blood and it felt so good to feel the essence of his spirit coursing through her veins. This is what he meant, when he spoke in that room a week ago, about the two of them becoming one. One mind, one heart, one soul first, then at the culmination of that process– one body.

"Pharaoh, can I ask you a question... about your business?" Cher asks lowly.

Pharaoh has been spending increasingly long hours at work. Yesterday he left the crib at 7am and did not come back until sometime after 11pm.

"Cher, what is the opposite of love?" Pharaoh asks calmly. He puts his fork down on the plate and places his elbows on the table. Pharaoh presses his fingertips together, as if conducting an interview.

"Hate," Cher answers astutely, but knowing that Pharaoh's question is not as simple as it appears.

"No, dear. The opposite of love is fear." His eyes darken as he expounds. "Perfect love casts out all fear."

Cher nods and files the information in her head. She knows now that she is being held responsible for knowing and understanding all that Pharaoh reveals to her.

"What is the opposite of darkness?" he asks curiously, like he doesn't know what answer he expects.

"Light," Cher responds, with the expectation of Pharaoh's correction.

"Knowledge," Pharaoh states plainly. "Only knowledge can fill the void of darkness. Light is a useless tool to overcome darkness without the knowledge of how to use it."

Cher nods, still not sure of how this exchange fits in with her original question.

"Ask me anything, Precious. You cannot love the Most High, if you fear him for lack of knowledge."

Maybe Cher should have found Pharaoh's god-like titles for himself disturbing, but she didn't. As the days pass, he has become increasingly obstinate about revealing his divine nature to her. Still, Pharaoh remains disarming, practical, loving, vulnerable, and very much human to her. She figures that his self-deification is more metaphorical or allegorical, than literal. But that's just because Cher doesn't yet know Pharaoh like I do.

"What do you do all day? What is your business comprised of?"

"Are you asking out of suspicion or for education?"

Cher was careful with her word choice. "I only want to know with whom I share My King."

Pharaoh smiles. He sees a sincerity in her that was not there before. She no longer compliments him. She adores him. She loves him and he can tell the difference now. She is not using her seduction on him. She is learning his ways and appealing to him with his own etiquette. She is his disciple.

"You goddess- do not share your god with anything or anyone. I am completely yours. As for my business, it is very complicated. I don't think that a woman could grasp its complexities."

"I don't seek to participate in it, just to better understand my King." Cher smiles.

"Hmmm..." Pharaoh wipes his mouth with a napkin and succumbs to her petition. It is important to him that she knows he will oblige her every request. It is integral to their trust that he keeps his word to her. Since Pharaoh's word is law, it cannot be trespassed, not even by the King himself.

"I am what you call an investor. I have meetings just about every day with all kinds of people who want my money. They sit around for hours, trying to impress me with fancy presentations and compelling summations of why I should give them my money. It's quite time-consuming, but that's basically what I do all day. I control large sums of money. I tell it where to go and it accomplishes many different purposes for many different people."

"If you spend so much money, how do you make money?" Cher asks hanging on his words.

"That is the principle behind wealth," his answers smoothly. "You have to spend money in order to make money. The more money you have in circulation the more wealth you can acquire."

Pharaoh sees that Cher isn't tracking with him. "Put it this way, remember those slot machines in Vegas?"
Cher nods.

"You know how people sit there pumping quarters into those machines all day long. Then after several hours, they hit the jackpot and win a hundred dollars. They feel good inside because they won, but they never consider the fact that they fed two hundred dollars in quarters to the machine. They come back again and put that same one hundred dollars back into the machine, this time they win it back and they feel like they accomplished something when in truth, they are still a hundred dollars in the red."

Cher nods along as Pharaoh continues, gesturing with his hands. Cher can tell he is a masterful business man; sharp-witted with an eloquent tongue. She wonders where he learned the art of negotiation.

"My business works on the opposite principle. I invest a certain amount of money in a company, let's say one dollar. Then I require three dollars in return for allowing them to use my one dollar. Out of the three dollars, I receive back, I take one of those dollars and invest it in another company, requiring the same three dollars of the other company. Now I'm six dollars up at the expense of only two dollars. As each company builds its profit margin, I continue to reap a benefit on that one dollar, despite the fact that I only paid out once. I own shares in many businesses around this area. I am L.A.'s version of Wall Street. Here in California, I am unmatched in the amount of weight I push around these streets." Pharaoh utters with pride.

"Okay," Cher proceeds cautiously. "What happens when people don't pay?"

Pharaoh senses that she is fishing for something.

"The truth is that I don't know what happens *if...* they don't pay. My clients always pay because they know they need what I have to offer. I do very honest business and I am very well respected, so people always pay- eventually. One way or the other, they always pay."

Cher probes a little further but changes directions, so as not to aggravate him. "You run a successful, legitimate business. So what's with the personal militia?"

"My men are some of my closest friends from the military. Musah saved my life once in Nam and I feel it's only fitting that he and others from my unit should share in the prosperity that I have found. My men are my business partners. I am not a hoodlum or a gangster. I don't shake people down, if that's what you think."

"No, I don't think that," Cher replies defensively.

"I am a very important man. My hand controls a lot of money. There are people who would like to take that money from me. My men are for my protection, a defense not an offense. President Ford has a legitimate office, but does he not have Secret Servicemen who are trained to defend him? With money comes power and I am god in LA. That's all you need to know and understand about my business." Pharaoh stands abruptly and leaves the table.

He finishes his morning preparations in the bedroom while Cher cleans the dishes from the meal.

"Cher," he says lightly, seemingly in a better mood when he enters the kitchen. "What do you want out of life?"

Cher stops scrubbing the pans at that question. She's never considered it before. She allows the words to slip effortlessly off her tongue. Her logic is the less she thinks about the question, the more honest her answer will be.

"Love... and Happiness."

"A tall order," Pharaoh replies instinctively, rubbing his chin. "You might as well have asked for the world, which you can still have if you want." Pharaoh ponders her request. "Love and Happiness. I think I can handle that," he says with finality. Pharaoh kisses her cheek, and then leaves the apartment.

****

By the time Pharaoh returns to his pad, he is physically exhausted. Cher has always seen him sharp and energetic all day, from before dawn until long after dusk. But on this evening, he shuffles into the apartment, heavy-footed and weary. Cher developed a bit of cabin-fever from being left alone in the penthouse, day after day. Since she began cooking dinner and Pharaoh approved of her culinary prowess, there were few excuses or occasions for her to leave the apartment. Cher went shopping down on Rodeo Drive a few times. She appreciated the fact that the White retail assistants were so courteous to her. They never watched her while she shopped or rushed her to make selections. They took their time with her, willing to pull out as many sizes or colors of anything that she wanted to try on.

When she placed the clothing on the counter, they would fold her items neatly and place them in designer bags. The retail lady would not so much as touch the cash register. When Cher would offer to pay, they would kindly advise her that it was not necessary and bid her a nice day. Cher knew how influential Pharaoh was, but how did they know her? She was beginning to feel like an invisible creature out of a science fiction movie. She figured it was Musah's presence always beside her, always to her right that must have alerted people that she was Pharaoh's woman. People could see Musah; tall, dark and handsome Musah. Everywhere he took Cher, people addressed him, sliding him skin and giving him almost the same respect as Pharaoh. Since people see Musah as a way to beg an audience of Pharaoh, he always seems to be engrossed in some manner of business at all times. Musah is definitely not a dumb, muscle-bound lackey in Pharaoh's servitude. He is an apt, intelligent lieutenant. Whenever approached, Musah was always careful to maintain some focus on Cher. Not like she was his prisoner to guard, but just a general cognizance of her movements and actions so that he could be ready to respond to whatever her request. Cher, on the other hand, never received any acknowledgement from anyone, unless in the capacity to accomplish her request.

People were polite and responsive to her, but not genial or personable. Even when she would ask an opinion of the assistants in the stores, they would just respond, "That's very lovely," or "I like that one, too." Cher wasn't sure if it was respect or intimidation that made people act the way they did around her, but she didn't like it. Even Musah refused to look her in the eye. He would wait at the entrance of the salons and stores for her, talking and conducting business with the owners or employees, glancing only occasionally in her general direction, but never actually at her. When she would try to strike up casual conversation with him, he would walk away as if she didn't say anything at all. Once she tried talking to him in the car, where he couldn't escape; but he just drove on, humming a tune as if in the car by himself. Only her requests were heeded by him and he was quick to complete them for her, but that was the extent of his interaction with her.

Cher stopped shopping. It made her too uncomfortable, plus she realized that no one would see her new outfits or care if they did. Pharaoh made it a point to compliment any new designer concoction that she whipped together, but most days he came home so late that he only got to see her in a night gown.

Cher had asked Pharaoh to take her to dinner, earlier that day; but by the look on his face, Cher could see that this was one request that Pharaoh would not be able to accomplish.

"No, no, no. If my goddess wants to go out, then we will," he sighs, as he drops down heavily onto the sofa. "Go get dressed, Mama. I'll be here when you're ready." He lays his head back against the cushions and closes his eyes.

"Pharaoh, I changed my mind," Cher says, letting him off the hook. "I want to stay in with you. I'll just order dinner. Are you feeling alright, My King?"

"I am tired. I don't know why, but I'm just *tired*," he breathes in astonishment. It seems this limitation has taken the wind out of Pharaoh's sails. Cher can tell that he hates to admit that anything other than his own will has mastered him today.

Cher kneels at Pharaoh's feet and removes his shoes and socks. She takes them to the bedroom, placing them on the left side of the closet, then takes a bottle of camphor and myrrh oil from his dresser. Cher has been increasingly accommodating to Pharaoh. He has become her whole world. He cares for her and attends to her every need and desire. Cher makes it her business, her full-time work, to conceive of ways to please him. Since physical intimacy is not in the routine for them, she has lots of energy to be creative in other ways. Cher comes breezing back into the room. Her black-silk, Oriental kimono with oversized sleeves flows as she walks. Her hair is done up in a smooth, polished up do. She went to the salon today, in anticipation of a night out with her Pharaoh.

"I apologize for not telling you how stunning you look, filet. I guess my fatigue is getting the best of me tonight."

"That's fine. Just so long as you appreciate the effort, because it's only and all for you."

Pharaoh doesn't seem convinced. His suspicion shows on his face.

"Are you a woman who needs lots of attention, Cher?" he asks inquisitively. She can tell this is an education question. Cher rubs the oil in her palms, heating it before taking Pharaoh's soft, pedicured foot in her hands.

"I don't know. I guess I've always had lots of attention, so I've never known what it's like to live without it."

"Until now," Pharaoh says perceptively. "Are you happy here? Is my adoration enough for you?"

"More than enough, my love." She is sincere. "I just get a little bored sometimes, that's all." She admits it because she knows that Pharaoh has already sensed it. She knows that the more open she is with him, the more he will trust her.

"Do you have any sisters or maybe a cousin that you would like me to bring out here to spend time with you?"

"No, I'm an only child." She caresses his feet. She can feel his muscles begin to relax. Pharaoh appreciates small gestures like this one from Cher. She does not do it often, but she doesn't have to. Pharaoh spends a few hours each week in a spa being pampered from head to tingly toe by his stylist, masseuse and manicurist. Still he appreciates the intimacy of having his woman desire to pleasure him... and pleasure him she does.

For the past few days, Pharaoh has been more aroused by Cher than ever. As she yields and submits to him, it makes him desire her more than he thought possible. He doesn't sleep with her anymore. He is concerned that his carnal nature may get the best of him and he take her love before she is ready.

"I, too, am an only child; so I can understand. Do you have some family that you would like to go and see? I will fly you anywhere you want to go. You are not a prisoner here."

Cher shakes her head. "I don't have any family- or friends even, I don't think." She pauses to ponder it. All of the stellas at the club would probably cut her throat in her sleep, if they had the chance. Cher didn't have even one close associate after she ran down the list of her acquaintances. "Nope. Just Cher. I don't even have a Big Mama like you."

Pharaoh seems surprised by her admission. "So Pharaoh is all Cher has in the world?"

Cher thought about it again, just to make sure. "Yeah, I guess so." She smiles.

"Well, who or what else could a girl need but Pharaoh?"

Cher shrugs her shoulders and laughs, stroking his ego as well as his feet.

"I will do better by you, mi amore. I will be all that you need," he promises solemnly. He leans forward and lightly kisses her lips.

134

"Tell Pharaoh what he can do for you. What would Her Majesty like from her King?"

"Can we go out this weekend?"

"Go out?" Pharaoh raises an eyebrow. "Be more specific."

"I want to dance," she gushes the words, laying her head longingly on his knee.

"Alright," Pharaoh says quietly, smoothing her hair. "Quoi que tu souhaites, ma cherie."

Although it is only Tuesday, Cher is so excited and thankful to Pharaoh for his devotion to her happiness. She has never seen him go out socially, so for him to commit to such an engagement is a huge act of selflessness on his part.

"Thank you, Papa!" She jumps into his lap. Pharaoh is overwhelmed as she pecks kisses on his face. He is overcome by her affection. Cher is innocent in her playfulness, but she is, unknowingly, releasing the lion in Pharaoh. He is fiercely loyal, so much so that he would never step out on Cher, not even enough to pleasure himself, so he is boiling to the surface with desire for her. Even the slightest enticement could send him over the edge that he feels himself slipping from when she hugs his neck.

"Okay, Mama," he says with a tone of resignation. He slides Cher from his lap, protecting his throbbing meat from the casual brush of her thigh. Pharaoh stands painfully and Cher is instantly concerned for him.

"What's wrong, Papa? You don't look so good." She watches his slow, limping steps.

"I'll be fine. I just need to lay down for a while. Call me when dinner arrives."

Once upstairs, Pharaoh does all he can to calm himself. He is on fire for Cher and all the meditation in the world cannot subdue it. He drops his pull out bed away from the wall and lays down fully-dressed. The blood pulsing violently through his manhood makes him lightheaded. He lays on his side and rubs the savage serpent to pacify his urges. Pharaoh tries to psyche himself out mentally so that he can rest; but just as his mind begins to clear of the seduction fog, an image of Cher appears before him.

She materializes in the doorway. The Isley Brothers cover of Bob Dillon's "Lay Lady Lay" is the record that Cher chose from his library and placed on the player. The music, like the light, flows around her silhouette and into the dark room where Pharaoh lays.

She is a vision of loveliness– a fantasy to him, when she enters the room. Her bare feet are silent on the padded floor. She is completely naked and Pharaoh is completely aroused, ready to respond to her every desire. He stands and steps over to meet her. His hands discover her nude body all over again, as if it is the first time. Cher can see that he is vulnerable, that he needs her love. His desperate need for her love has weakened him and she knows it. She wants to invigorate her King and give him back his radiance.

She lets her hands slip up his neck and into his hair, as his lips find hers. His hands rub down her back and over her hips as his manhood shows his appreciation for her presence. Cher pulls out the pins, securing her up do and her hair cascades down over her back. Pharaoh buries his face in her hair. She smells sweet, the fragrant oils on her skin enchant Pharaoh's senses. He feels her soft breasts and firm nipples against his stomach, as they kiss long and slow.

Cher takes the lead, feeling that her wilted king may need her assistance. She unbuttons his shirt, but he grips her wrists before she can make much progress. He pushes her down onto the bed. Cher sees her King of the Jungle, her regal lion regaining his resilience. He pops the buttons, ripping the shirt open to reveal his heaving, hairy chest. Pharaoh's eyes burn with passion. He unbuckles his leather belt and wraps it around his hand. He whips it in the air before letting it drop to the floor. Cher is exhilarated by the Lioness Tamer that stands before her. She wants him to subdue the wild beast within her and dominate her body like no other man has.

As she lays before him with her legs spread wide, revealing her juicy pink opening to him, Pharaoh hesitates. He drops his pants, but stands as if suspended in space.

"Do you want this?... To be one with me?" He asks gently. His lips are moist, as he steps out of his briefs. He stands over Cher gently stroking his manhood, which bucks and drools in his hand like a vicious attack dog held only by a thin, fraying leash.

Cher is so seduced by the drop of clear fluid that leaks from the tip. She knows that he is boiling over inside for her.

"Yes, Pharaoh. Make me one with you. Make love to me."

Pharaoh smiles at her request. He wasn't prepared to resist if she hadn't consented. Cher is ready for him to mount her. She positions herself against the pillows, but instead of climbing on the bed, Pharaoh goes into the closet. He comes back shortly with something in his hand. He slinks down beside Cher in the bed. She studies his face, as he turns the object over in his hand.

"Do you trust your King, Cher?"

"Yes," she breathes, staring into his beautiful, black eyes.

"Do you believe that I would ever hurt you?"

"No," Cher answers sincerely.

"Well tonight I am going to hurt you," he says solemnly. Cher is confused by his confession. "In addition to the pain you will feel, I am going to take something that you've never given up before."

Cher feels panic creep into her limbs as he speaks. "My manhood and my life are two different things. I have put my dick inside of women before, but I have not given any of them my life. I want you to have that from me, Cher. My life inside of you."

Cher is sure she doesn't know what he is talking about so she listens carefully, quelling the throbbing in her chocha so she can focus.

"I don't want to make fierce love to you. Your body cannot handle that yet. I want to make slow, patient love to you. I want to take my time with you, so that you understand me when we are done." Cher nods and breathes slowly, she wants to concentrate on his words.

"In order for me to put my life inside of you, I will have to take yours. Do you understand?"
Cher shakes her head.

"I know you don't understand and I know that you may never completely understand, so your understanding is not required." Cher blinks long, her mind suddenly feels like a pretzel.

"I just need to know that you trust me," he says, holding up his long, pointer finger. "Do you trust me with your life, Cher?"

Cher nods. "Yes, Papa. I trust you," she whispers solemnly. Pharaoh watches her eyes. His stare shifts from one eye to the other. Cher's expression is soft and innocent like a child. He knows she is telling him what she believes to be the truth.

"Do you know why I chose you for my goddess, Cher? Do you know what makes you worthy over any other female to have my life inside of you?"

That was a question that always made her wonder. Cher knew she was a knockout, but she was a stripper and Pharaoh didn't seem like the type of man to consort with her element. She wondered daily why he had brought her home with him when he could have had any woman he wanted. She didn't think she was beneath him, but just from a different lifestyle. There never seemed to be a logical reason for him to choose her for his mate.

After careful consideration, Cher shakes her head.

"Before I went to Vegas, I had a dream; a beautiful dream of a beautiful woman. The woman in the dream was a constellation. High above my pyramid, her light gave life and energy to her god and to his temple compound. When I saw you at the Lounge shining like a silver star, I recognized you immediately; exactly the same vision that I had seen in my dream. I didn't even waste the time of watching you because I knew that you were mine. I knew that I was there that night, solely for the purpose of meeting you. Our meeting was foretold and predestined. Somewhere on the walls of an ancient pyramid, there are pictures of us– you and me- as hieroglyphic images, enthroned in gold."

Pharaoh turns the heat back up on a conversation that was beginning to leave Cher cold. His morbid, cryptic talk about trust and life alarmed her. She thought at one point that she should just get dressed and go back downstairs, but as he spoke on she realized that Pharaoh's love for her was connected to a deeper epiphany than she understood. If she trusted him like she said she did, she would have to believe that he had an insight into the ethereal and she would have to put her confidence in him to impart it to her as their life together unfolds.

Pharaoh kisses her lips, interrupting her meditation.

"Do you trust me, goddess?"
Cher isn't sure what Pharaoh's precepts refer to but, somewhere deep inside, they resonate; answering a lifelong question in her soul and resolving the breach in her heart. She

knows looking in Pharaoh's eyes that he will never leave her. He will protect her and love her with his all.

"Yes," she says assuredly.

"Now I want to worship you with my body, the way I have with my heart and soul."

Pharaoh stretches a satin sash between both hands. Cher lifts her head and Pharaoh blindfolds her. He shrouds her face completely, allowing the fabric to drape down over her chin. Cher breathes slowly beneath it, apprehensive about what comes next.

Pharaoh's lips descend on her sporadically, in a light staccato rhythm, like rain. He kisses her there, and there, and there... and then... right there. He runs his tongue from here to there. Pharaoh's long, sucking kisses stimulate her limbs, making it difficult for Cher to tell what body part they are on. Cher moans and sucks in a deep hissing breath. The satin blindfold sticks to her moistened lips. Her body feels electrified, charged with ecstasy, as his tongue conducts a symphony of sensations.

Next comes a touch, light and soft like a feather, tingling and tickling her skin. He traces her body even to the soles of her feet. She flinches slightly and giggles when the feather brushes over her knees. Pharaoh's love, in the dark anticipation of the blindfold, is heightened by the elimination of her primary sense. Cher is taken by surprise over and over again, unable to predict his next exhilarating move. Cher gasps with expectancy. Pharaoh gently persuades Cher's love to come down, sucking on each of her toes. She sighs heavily, as a warm puddle forms between her legs. Pharaoh is satisfied with his progress. He parts her knees to see the moist petals, glistening in the faint light outside the bedroom. He crawls between her welcoming thighs and lays against her stomach, before loosening the sash.

"Are you ready?" he whispers on her lips, his breath so sweet that Cher can taste it in her mouth. "This won't be comfortable for you, goddess."

Cher nods nervously and closes her eyes. Pharaoh moistens the tip of his organ in her nectar. She holds her breath when she feels the pressure of his manhood against the entrance to her love. He taps gently but the door will not open to him. Pharaoh pushes hard against her taunt flesh. Cher whimpers a little when he bursts through her barricade.

"Are you okay, Love?" he whispers softly into her ear.

"Mmm hmm," Cher nods, wincing as he presses gently. Pharaoh squeezes her buttocks tightly, breathing heavy against her neck. Cher lets the cool metal of Pharaoh's gold chains laying against her chest distract her from the discomfort. A low growl slips from Pharaoh lips when he slides deep inside of her. Cher is ecstatic, feeling Pharaoh's love pulsing inside of her. His strokes are long and slow at first. Cher begins to purr as the pain dissipates and is replaced by a magnificent tingling sensation that radiates throughout her hips. Pharaoh clutches the bottom of her thighs and lifts them, creating a little more space for his manhood to probe her warm, wet femininity. She can feel the force of him plunging and diving inside of her. She is so overcome with the thrill of his love. Pharaoh is long and strong and it shows in the thrust of his hips.

Cher licks her lips, as his hand rubs along her body. Cher feels a faint tremble in Pharaoh's body, as he glides inside of her. He is overcome with her love. The experience is more glorious than he could have ever imagined in his wildest fantasies. Her tight flesh hugs his manhood, sucking and pulling on him like a mouth. Her love is custom made for his body, like his suits, even the way his waist fits between her thighs is perfect. His pelvis rubs over her clitoris, heightening her stimulation. He is deep enough inside of Cher to quake the earth for her, and when he feels a gentle quiver traveling through her thighs he knows he is hitting the mark.

"Oh, Pharaoh," she moans, gripping his shoulders so tightly that her nails dig in. Pharaoh folds her legs around his waist and wraps her arms tightly around his neck. He lifts Cher off the bed with his elbows under her knees. His love still throbs inside of her while he kisses her lips passionately. He presses her back firmly against the wall, causing Cher to sigh under his weight. Pharaoh begins to probe her again. His stroke is so long that Cher thinks it will never end. Her discomfort intensifies in that position. Her moans turn to whines when he presses his manhood deeper inside of her love. Cher wants to ask Pharaoh to stop, but she knows how patiently he has waited to experience her body, so she wants him to get his fill of her.

Cher didn't even expect it when it came. She was in the middle of breathing deeply, trying to tolerate and subside the pain, when it sneaked up and surprised her– a hot, gushing climax explodes inside of her. Pharaoh's persistence prevails and Cher cums so hard that her body rocks against the wall from the intensity of her orgasm. She wails loudly and convulses while Pharaoh drags her pleasure out, pressing down deep into her tight, saturated femininity.

Pharaoh lowers Cher's feet gently to the ground. The throbbing between her legs feels so painfully sweet, sending pleasure ripples throughout her body when she presses her thighs together.

"Bow down before your god." Pharaoh places his hand on her shoulder. Pharaoh has dominated Cher's mind, spirit, heart and finally her body. She knows now that she belongs completely to him and she wants to. He is magnificent to her. His love is more than she could have hoped for. Cher had never shared the experience of an orgasm with a man before she met Pharaoh and aside from the ones she had induced herself, didn't think it was possible for her to feel that way. Pharaoh's love exceeded what she could accomplish on her own. The feeling of his manhood still tingled painfully warm inside of her loins. He had made her one with him.

Even as he stands before her, Cher feels them breathing in time with each other, as if it is only one breath that they share between the two of them. As he exhales, she inhales and the transfer is complete. She kneels slowly in front of him. His long, thick organ pulses beside her face.

"Receive my life from me. Take the gift that your King offers to you." Pharaoh presses his thumb against her chin, dropping her jaw open. Pharaoh slips his manhood between her lips. He holds the back of her head and plunges what he can fit deep into her mouth. Cher moans, surprised by the ecstasy of his love sliding over her tongue. She opens wide, allowing him to enjoy her mouth, and use the space however it pleases him. Her hands massage his powerful thighs. The veins in his manhood thump wildly, begging for the release. Pharaoh begins to gently caress his shaft, encouraging the ejaculation to come forth. His body tenses and he begins to exhale heavily when the cum erupts on to Cher's tongue. The thick, warm secretion floods her mouth and runs down her cheek.

"Drink it all," he commands, rubbing his manhood. Cher swallows hard and licks the remnant off of her lips.

"Good goddess." He pats her head. Pharaoh takes Cher's hand and helps her to her feet. He hugs her tightly, signifying that he approves of her love.

"Are you pleased with me, my King?" She asks eagerly. She longs desperately for his affirmation. Cher is not even sure why, but she is so completely his now that all she wants is to satisfy him.

"Yes. Very much, goddess. Your love is Supreme." He smiles at her. Pharaoh runs his fingers though her hair and brushes his lips against her cheek. "I love you, goddess."

The admission shocks Cher at first, then she feels the warmth of his words heating up her heart.

"I love you too, Pharaoh," she says shyly, covering her smile with her hands. It feels like a dream to exchange those words with him. Cher hugs his waist and kisses his chin.

She releases him reluctantly, then limps over to the bathroom. Cher had no idea at the time that Pharaoh's love was doing so much damage- but she did survive it and discovered that there was nothing to be afraid of. Even in the midst of the pain, she still found his sex to be delightfully masterful.

Pharaoh, observing her discomfort, instructs her. "Cher, draw a warm bath and add two cups of lemon juice. That will stop the pain and help you recover."

# FOR THE LOVE OF MONEY

The following morning, it became apparent to Cher why Pharaoh had such a vested interest in her speedy recovery.

He was back to himself, as invigorated and energetic as ever. He woke her up extremely early with his love. He was like a young, ravenous lion. He changed his routine to start his day with her love before his morning martial artistry.

Cher was so drained and sore afterwards that she could not leave the bed to prepare his breakfast. Which was fine, Pharaoh didn't mind one bit. He prepared breakfast in bed for her instead and catered to Cher even more than his usual efforts.

As the days passed, Cher came to understand what Pharaoh meant when he said that the privilege of his love came with great responsibility. He was completely insatiable. He would take her at *least* twice daily. Not satisfied to pleasure just himself, he would not stop until Cher gave him the offering of her climax as well. She couldn't complain. Pharaoh never let it become mundane or predictable. Between his mouth and his manhood, Cher experienced more ecstasy from Pharaoh than she knew was possible.

Thursday, he rang the phone in the apartment and told Cher he was coming home for lunch. She prepared a light meal for him but, when he came through the door, food was not what he desired. Instead of sitting at the table, he bent Cher over it and took her from behind. Too aroused to undress, he lifted her skirt around her waist and pulled down her underwear. He pressed his love passionately inside of her, gripping the back of her neck tightly with one hand and her hip with the other. He wasn't satisfied until he made her holler with pleasure and beg him to stop.

By Saturday morning, Pharaoh was satiated enough to give Cher the morning off. He didn't even bother her with breakfast. He let her stir on her own around 10am.

"Good morning, goddess," he beams, softly kissing her lips.

"Good morning, my King," she whispers hoarsely.

Pharaoh hands her the large mug of warm, green tea that he was drinking. "Thank you, Papa," she says before taking a long, slow sip.

"I am sending you to the spa today," he begins simply. "You are to spend the entire day, so I need the apartment key."

Cher takes the chain from around her neck and places it in Pharaoh's hand.

"I have given implicit directions concerning you. You are to have whatever you want. They will massage, soak, steam and pamper you until you feel like a newborn baby. I want you to unwind before our night out on the town."

Cher was so exhausted from the week that she had almost forgotten about their plans. The fatigue melts, as she smiles and nods at him. Pharaoh smiles back, happy to impress his woman with his reliability.

"Get dressed and Benny will take you when you are ready?"

"What about Musah?" Cher asks quickly.

"What about Musah?" Pharaoh's eyes squint and sharpen.

Cher instantly regrets her question. "It's just that he is my usual escort, so I didn't know if maybe something happened to him."

By the expression on Pharaoh's face, Cher knows she can't salvage this mistake. Finally, she understands the reason why Musah treats her the way he does. Pharaoh eye-stalks Cher like a wild animal in a cage.

"Are you fond of Musah? Would it please you if I had him take you to the spa, instead of Benny?"

"No, Pharaoh. That's not what I meant and you know it."

"All I know is what you tell me, goddess."

"Well, I am telling you that it will be fine for Benny or Blaze or whomever *you* designate to take me to the spa."

Pharaoh resigns from the brewing confrontation. He is more patient than he was when he and I were married. He makes the internal decision to take Musah off Cher detail. He will find more productive work for him.

Cher and Musah are the two closest people to him in the world, so for now, he will give them the benefit of the doubt. He is going to watch them as close as a hawk though, and they had better hope that not even the semblance of betrayal surfaces.

Pharaoh's love for Cher is something different than I have ever seen from him. He truly wants to be an immaculate lover to her, but infidelity, whether emotional or physical, is something that Pharaoh will not tolerate from any woman.

"Get relaxed and beautiful for tonight. I have many meetings today, so I will see you later, goddess." Pharaoh speaks sweetly to her. He even kisses her neck softly, as he wraps his arms around her waist and squeezes her gently. Cher appreciates his embrace and his forgiveness. She hopes that his anger has truly subsided. She has learned over time how territorial and possessive Pharaoh can be. Cher thinks it's charming- but at the same time, she never wants the coin to flip.

****

Cher spent the day being pressed... and pulled... and stroked... and rubbed. The masseuse caressed Cher's body from scalp to toe until her whole being tingled with numbness. The esthetician placed cucumber slices over her eyes and spread an avocado mask over her face. The multiple female attendants scrubbed Cher's body with sea salts and wrapped her, shoulder to foot, in plastic like a leftover rump roast. After she lay in a warm, sauna room to sweat for an hour, she was taken into a shower, rinsed clean and toweled dried; only to be placed into a tub full of warm mud. At first Cher was disgusted by the idea of it. The mud didn't stink or anything. It was actually quite fragrant, but just the consistency of it was enough to turn her stomach. Cher was afraid of getting it up inside of her. However, after a half-hour of soaking in it, Cher didn't want to leave. Her limbs felt heavy with relaxation, so much so that she could not sit comfortably for her manicure and pedicure. Cher leaned in the chair while the stylist straightened her hair. None of them dared tell her to hold her head up. They just worked as best they could around her dangling head, trying not to burn her.

Cher was so inebriated with gratification when she left the spa that she was unsteady on her feet. She almost wanted to ask Benny to carry her to the car, but she knew better. She laid across the back seat as he drove, and although the apartment was just a few blocks away, she was sound asleep when they arrived. It was late in the afternoon, so Pharaoh wrapped up his meetings when Benny called him from the spa to say they were on their way back to the apartment.

Cher is so beautiful to him. Pharaoh smiles when he opens the car door to find her curled up like a child; fast asleep on the back seat. Pharaoh scoops Cher up into his arms. She barely stirs. She has no idea where she is or who is carrying her, neither does she care as she lays heavy against Pharaoh's chest. He takes her up in the elevator and lays her in the bed, then closes the door behind him.

When Cher wakes a few hours later, her muscles are stiff, but she feels refreshed and rejuvenated. She had no idea how much tension was stored up in her body. Pharaoh slips back into the room when he hears her stirring in the bed.

"Did you rest well, goddess?" he asks, turning on a dim red-bulb lamp.

Cher nods sleepily, musing at the sight of her foxy Pharaoh.

He looks stunningly simple, wearing a long, red Caftan over denim bell bottoms.

"If you didn't want to go out tonight, all you had to do was say so." Cher smiles, pushing herself to a seated position. "You didn't have to have me drugged like a wild animal."

Pharaoh laughs gently. He hands her a glass of water, then sits down on the foot of the bed.

"I've been meaning to send you for a while now. I just kept forgetting to make the arrangements. It won't be so debilitating once you get used to it. Tension is like poison to the body. When the toxins are released, they can have an adverse effect at first, but I'm sure you feel better now."

"Yes, I do," Cher sighs in amazement. She yawns and stretches her arms over her head. "I can't believe how good I feel. I feel... invincible."

"That's because you are, goddess." Pharaoh brushes her cheek with his thumb. "Let's get ready to book, Mama. We're going out to dinner before we hit the Sunset strip. I'm taking my foxy to **The Roxy**," Pharaoh says playfully.

"Sounds fun," Cher replies optimistically, trying to muster up her energy.

****

**The Roxy** is live and packed wall-to-wall with people; some dancing on the floor, others on raised platforms in disco, psychedelic outfits. The scene is live. It is like **Soul Train**, but with more White people. Pharaoh refused to let Cher out of the house in her silver mini-skirt, so she settled on a sexy, emerald green halter neck, wide-legged cat suit under her striped black and gray full-length Chinchilla fur coat– a new present from Pharaoh. The only thing heavier than her coat was the weight in diamonds on her neck and wrists.

### Pharaoh Forever

They are showstoppers in the club. Pharaoh, not outdone by his woman, gleams from head-to-toe in white and gold. From his white, wide-brimmed fedora with a gold feather, to his white Cortelle trouser suit with gold buttons, to his white open neck shirt with gold cufflinks, down to his white gator boots with gold soles. Pharaoh looks as angelic as Saint Peter, his full-length white leather jacket spreading like wings when he walks.

They don't break their stride, getting out of the Cadillac curbside and walking past the line of freezing cats waiting to get into the club. Benny, Blaze, Musah and Jinx were all on hand for this occasion. Two in front and two at the rear, the crowd parts as Pharaoh and Cher cruise straight in and across the dance floor to the VIP lounge at the back of the building. The room is reserved exclusively for the two of them and once they are inside, Musah closes the door tightly. The wall of the room that faces the dance floor is completely glass, so Cher loves it. She is able to watch the party people and hear the thumping, heart-pounding music without having to dance amongst the crowd. In the VIP lounge, she can dance freely and not worry about being bumped or groped. Cher's feet begin to shuffle instantly, as the silver and gold flashing lights inspire her groove. Before she can get her full-fledged twist and shout going, Pharaoh draws the heavy, purple velvet curtain across the wall of the VIP room.

In the center of the room is a pole that extends up to the ceiling from a table platform with champagne, candies and flute glasses. Pharaoh removes the tray, placing it on an end table.

"Now, you dance for me... and only me," he says seductively, taking off his hat and sitting down onto the soft, velvet sofa in front of her. Cher smiles, then climbs on the platform and leans back against the pole. She is excited to work it for her man, but the added bonus is that they are playing her song.

"I... love to love you, baby..."

She circles the platform, strutting slowly and seductively for Pharaoh. Suddenly, Cher swings around the pole with her legs extended in a V, descending until her bottom touches down. Cher lays backwards, letting her head and shoulders drape over the edge of the platform. Her hair hangs down to the floor and she watches Pharaoh upside down.

"I love to love you, baby..."

Cher reaches out for him, running her hand along the inside of his thigh. She whips her body back up to a seated position. She brings her legs together and rises slowly, poking out her rear end for Pharaoh to get his eyeful. She glances over her shoulder at him, gathering her hair in her hands and pulling it forward over one shoulder. Pharaoh rubs the expanding mass that swells along the inside of his thigh, as she reveals the soft, glowing skin of her back to him.

Cher learned from years of being a mediocre exotic dancer that men are more turned on by the simplest features on a woman like the nape of her neck, her scent, her shoulders, her eyelashes, her ankles– even more than being able to see down to her ovaries. Those basic broads in the club didn't get that. They would damn near kill themselves trying to turn a trick. Cher never shared her secret with those barracudas. Sure, Cher is stunning in the face with a body to match, but none of that really matters. There are plenty of beautiful women in the world and all men like different things- but the one thing they have in common is that they **all** appreciate the *femininity* of a woman. Men are made that way– to desire what is soft and vulnerable. It is Cher's subtle, kitten-like ways that men find so alluring. That's what sets her apart from so many other females.

Pharaoh breathes deeply, watching her through intensely focused eyes. Cher reaches up to the collar of her halter and loosens the clasp. She turns to face Pharaoh and lowers the front of her cat suit, exposing her silky breasts to him. At that point, unable to contain his passion any longer, Pharaoh stands up from his seat. He grabs Cher's waist and pulls her off the platform. Pharaoh sits back down with her straddling his lap. She runs her hands over his muscular shoulders. Cher can feel his arousal between her buttocks. Pharaoh leans Cher back and gently sucks on her nipples.

"You smell so good," he whispers, lifting her neck up to his lips. "Mmm," he moans, kissing the parts of her collarbone that are not covered with jewels. "Your skin is so soft."

Cher unbuttons his trousers and takes his love into her hands. She kneels between his legs and presses her breasts together. She rubs them along his manhood. Pharaoh groans, pushing his pelvis forward. Cher licks the head each time it pokes up from between her breasts. Just as she is about to take him into her mouth, the lounge door cracks slightly– just a thin line of light appears on the floor in the dim room.

"Boss, it's important," is all that Musah squeezes through the tiny opening, before swiftly jerking the door closed.

"Goddess," Pharaoh sighs his disappointment while struggling to tuck his manhood back into his pants. "We will finish this in a minute, but for now enjoy yourself in here until I return."

Cher fastens the top of her halter while Pharaoh adjusts himself before leaving the room. Pharaoh had been thoughtful enough to have a bottle of ginger ale for her, so she pours a flute and relaxes on the sofa. She even boogies down a bit, before Pharaoh comes bursting through the door.

"We gotta' book on up outta here, Cher," he says with quiet

calm, while gathering up their belongings.

"It's still early, Papa," she whines.

"We are going... **now**."

Pharaoh's demeanor is still cool, but his tone is cold. Cher doesn't question him further. She slips back into her platform sandals and pushes her arms into her fur. Pharaoh takes Cher's hand and leads her out of the club, following close behind Jinx and Blaze. Musah and Benny are already out front sitting curbside when they exit the front doors.

Pharaoh and Cher climb into the back seat of the Cadillac. Pharaoh wraps his arm around Cher's shoulders, holding her tightly to him. Cher enjoys the gentle warmth of his embrace. Usually they ride, side-by-side with only the contact of their knees rubbing together or Cher places her hand on his while it rests in his lap.

What Cher is mistaking for affection is actually protection. Pharaoh isn't telling her any of the reasons why they are leaving the club. In Cher's mind, Pharaoh is eager for her love and doesn't want any more interruptions.

Pharaoh scans the scene, as he usually does when they are driving along. The car is completely silent, not even the radio plays, only the smooth, crisp sound of the tires on the pavement. Musah turns off of the strip and cuts down through a long, dark alleyway. They cruise slowly between the buildings, then emerge on a dark back street.

Cher hadn't noticed anything at first. She figured it was business as usual like it always is. Maybe Pharaoh was being called into a night meeting, as he is from time to time. But then Cher finally detects it– the thick, stifling tension in the air. She even realizes that they aren't taking the same route back to the apartment that they took coming to the club. Musah seems to be navigating the streets like a maze, turning right and left, then left and right again, almost doubling back a couple of times.

Cher can see the concern in Pharaoh's eyes when he locks in on something through the back window of the car. Whatever it is has Benny and Musah's attention as well, as they peer periodically into the side and rearview mirrors. Cher developed street smarts from being an orphan. She can feel a sense of foreboding, creeping under her skin, prickling up the hairs on the back of her neck.

Musah pulls up to a blinking red stoplight on a narrow street, heading towards an underpass that leads to the highway. When the car comes to a halt, Cher hears tires screeching, as three cars pull alongside the Cadillac. She doesn't hear the gunshots yet, only the sound of the driver side window shattering right before Musah slumps across the armrest. Then a barrage of bullets is pumped into the left side of the car. Shells shower down like rain as the gunmen unload on the vehicle. Cher doesn't have a chance to scream before Pharaoh grabs her around the neck and pulls her down on the floor of the Cadillac.

"Get down," he commands loudly, pressing on her back. Cher buries her head. Pharaoh reaches over the front seat to Musah. Benny throws open his door and crawls along the passenger side of the car. He places his back against the tire so that he can survey the scene and ensure the right side of the car is clear. Benny begins to return fire across the hood of the Cadillac with his .357 Magnum. Pharaoh joins the gun fight after breaking out the back window of the car with the hilt of Musah's gold-plated Beretta. Suddenly, a fifth car, Pharaoh's Monte Carlo, comes charging in, crashing into the enemy Cutlass Supreme and pinning two gunmen against the doors. Jinx and Blaze step out boldly, firing incessantly on the men. Pharaoh and Benny are accurate with their shots too and– with some artillery assistance from two more of Pharaoh's men on the roof of an abandoned liquor store– within seconds the blaze of gunfire is diminished to a few random pops.

Pharaoh kicks open the mangled Cadillac door. It twists on the hinges and squeals loudly when he slams it closed behind him. Cher listens to the steps on the pavement; his heels scrunching in broken glass. Once she believes that Pharaoh is far enough away, she lifts her head just enough to peek out of the shattered car window. Pharaoh and Benny walk across the street to where the enemy gunmen lay, scattered on the ground around their vehicles. Pharaoh's leather jacket whips in the wind, as the small army of his men gather to him. Pharaoh's eyes are dark; his pupils so large that his entire eye turns black. Cher can see them clearly under the glow of the streetlights. She is more terrified by his face than she had been of the entire ordeal. Pharaoh transforms into a creature so hideous, Cher prays for the strength to forget what she is witnessing. She hopes she will not see this ghastly face when she looks into eyes of her sweet, gentle Pharaoh.

Pharaoh's men stand down. They remain shoulder to shoulder in a barricade behind him. Cher can still see Pharaoh. He is almost a whole head taller than all of them. Cher realizes as she looks around that Pharaoh is not on the defense and not the least bit surprised by the outcome of this engagement. He has eliminated the threat with quite an impressive counter offensive attack plan of his own.

Pharaoh had Musah lure the cars to this narrow area, giving the rooftop snipers the opportunity to mow the men down without giving them any avenue of escape. Blaze and Jinx were set up to tail the cars that were following Pharaoh and serve as a secondary wave of the cavalry. The plan was sheer military genius.

The street is completely desolate in a slum part of town. There are no sirens in the distance, no onlookers on the sidewalk, and no signs of life anywhere on this tiny, destitute piece of pavement.

Only sad, abandoned buildings slouching along either side of the street can serve as witnesses to this gunfight. The busy highway looms overhead; but down here under the overpass, it is a ghost town.

Pharaoh's men stand in the street, watching two of their adversaries struggling, even in the hopelessness of the situation, to get to their guns. One of the men, a young, dark-skinned, smooth-faced Brother manages to scramble to his feet. He stands before Pharaoh, panting and wheezing with blood pouring from his mouth and chest. The man is in pain, but his sharp, dark eyes are clear. He puffs up his chest with pride, proclaiming to Pharaoh, in an unspoken language, that he is ready to die for his cause.

Pharaoh gives him a sympathetic look, poking out his bottom lip before he raises the gun to his face. The gold pistol gleams in the light, like Pharaoh is holding fire in his left hand. Pharaoh pulls the trigger slowly, feeling ecstasy like an orgasm when the gun explodes in his hand. The force from the trajectory of the bullet at point blank range splits the man's head apart like a ripe melon. Pharaoh doesn't even blink when the flesh splatters in his face. Pharaoh licks the drops of warm, salty blood from his lips, as the man's body slumps to the ground. Pharaoh steps over him and crosses to another man who is in much worse condition. The man still slithers painfully on the ground, pulling himself along by one arm. He reaches for a gun, just as Pharaoh's boot comes down on the back of his hand. The man gurgles out a muffled yelp through the blood in his mouth when Pharaoh grinds his heel into the bones, breaking his hand.

"Turn over," Pharaoh quietly commands the husky, chestnut-complexioned man, nudging his ribs with the tip of his bloody boot.

The man flips over on his back, clutching his hand and staring up at Pharaoh with fear in his eyes. He is so terrified that his breaths come too fast and he begins to cough up blood. Pharaoh pumps two rounds into the man's left knee. The sound of the bones ripping apart can be heard over the gunfire. On the third trigger pull, the slide locks back. The Beretta is empty.

Pharaoh glances over to his militia. Five stone faces watching him stoically with crossed arms. Pharaoh tosses Jinx the Berretta and Jinx tosses Pharaoh his Browning Hi-Power 9mm. Pharaoh catches the gun gracefully, then fires bullets into the man until there is little more than a puddle where his knees should be.

The man is too weak to scream or cry. He lays trembling and whimpering on the ground. His breaths quicken to an erratic pace, when Pharaoh stoops down beside him. Pharaoh sighs heavily, like the exhale after a long drag from a cigarette. He rests his elbows on his thighs and lets his hands drop down between his knees.

Pharaoh has to calm himself. Killing makes him giddy. He hates to admit it, but this is his favorite guilty pleasure. Better even than sex or money. Pharaoh, in his attempt to civilize and enlighten himself, replaced his ardor for murder with business endeavors. Pharaoh works so hard to keep the assassin in him asleep. But on nights like this- when the scent of death hangs so heavy in the air, he feels like an invincible warrior. Pharaoh feels like a gladiator champion, as he inspects his white suit that is covered in the blood of his enemies.

"This is a lucky night for you, my friend... Pharaoh is in the mood to forgive." Pharaoh touches his right hand to his chest.

"I have a job for you. I want you to work for me now." He speaks softly and sincerely to the man. "I, Pharaoh, would never send you into a death trap like this against a god who cannot be killed. Pharaoh does not require sacrifice... only *obedience*."

Pharaoh holds up his long, pointer finger.

"You can obey Pharaoh and live-" He turns up his right palm. "Or rebel against Pharaoh and die." He turns up his left hand with the gun in it. "The choice is yours, my friend. Pharaoh does not force the allegiance of anyone."

The man nods frantically, more from his body going into shock, than the physical willing of his head to move.

"Okay. My request is simple. Tell your old boss that Pharaoh is not a man who can be killed. Pharaoh is god in LA and there is none other..."

Cher hears Musah begin to pant. He is still lying motionless and she is concerned that he may die, but she knows that she might be next if Pharaoh finds her touching him. When Cher sees Pharaoh heading back towards the Cadillac, she lays flat against the floorboard.

Pharaoh swings the car door open and begins to issue commands like a general. "Jinx, Johnny and Action-" Pharaoh points the men out. "You three get Musah in the Monte Carlo and take him out to my house. Call my doctor for him." Action takes the keys from Jinx, then the three men strenuously pull the Cadillac door open and strain to heave Musah's large body out of the driver's seat.

"Benny, you take Cher and follow them in the Imperial." He takes the keys to his Imperial from Action and tosses them to Benny. Cher notices a large blood stain on Pharaoh's right arm, different from the other small splatter drops.

"Baby, they shot you," she cries hysterically, grabbing his hand. Pharaoh looks down at his arm, in amazement. He hadn't noticed the gunshot wound in his shoulder, but sure enough, he is bleeding right through his jacket.

"Be still, woman," Pharaoh whispers forcefully in her ear. He holds her hands tightly together to stop them from shaking. "Your god cannot die." He assures her with steady eyes. "Now go!"

Cher follows Benny, but glances back over to Pharaoh and Blaze, who are checking the Cadillac to see if it can be driven. Everyone jumps into each of the three vehicles and screech off in different directions, all headed for the same destination–somewhere north of LA...

# THE BIG PAYBACK

Pharaoh and Blaze are last to pull up at the house in Echo Park around 1am.

They whip into the long winding, cobblestone driveway pushing a completely different car. One of Pharaoh's beneficiaries happens to be a Car Lot/ Salvage Yard. He was able to have the Cadillac destroyed and traded out for a brand new, tan-leather interior, pearl-colored Rolls Royce. Pharaoh and Benny had to ditch their bloodied clothes, so the car was not the only thing they changed. Pharaoh stepped out of the passenger seat looking as fresh as new money in a dark green leisure suit, with so much jewelry hanging from his wrists he looked like he was melting gold.

Pharaoh and Blaze trot up the gray, split-finish granite steps to the heavy double doors at the front of his spacious four-bedroom house. The grand, white house is immaculate with four huge, ivory pillars along the front. The house sits way up high on a hill facing away from the city and overlooking a pond. A large in-ground pool and Jacuzzi tub sit between the main house and an accommodating guesthouse on the east side of the estate. The lush, green grounds are completely surrounded by a tall, iron security fence. Only Pharaoh knows the gate code and he changes it almost daily. Once he and Blaze are inside, he changes it again, so that even his men won't be able to reenter once they leave.

"Where is Cher?" Pharaoh asks hurriedly when Jinx opens the front door for him.

"She's upstairs in the master bedroom," he reports directly. "She is fine."

"And Musah?" Pharaoh strides swiftly past the congregation of his men in the living room on his left. He walks straight across the black-and-white marble, checkerboard foyer to a door underneath the double staircase with gold railings. The small white, wooden door looks as if it belongs to an ordinary coat closet; but once inside of the closet, there is an inner door made of steel which opens to a short stairwell.

"Musah is not fine," Jinx replies solemnly, following Pharaoh and Blaze down the stairs to yet another steel door. Pharaoh knocks and the thin, eye slit on the door slides back, revealing a set of slender, squinty black eyes. The locks turn with a heavy click and then the door swings open for Pharaoh and his company.

"What's the status?" Pharaoh asks the young, African doctor with genuine concern in his tone. Pharaoh walks to the back of the vast basement. Action, Johnny and Benny are there. They look nervously at Pharaoh, biting their lips and covering their mouths with their hands.

Benny paces angrily. He is almost as pale with grief as Musah. He can't help but wish he could have done more for his friend. He would have taken the bullet for Musah if he could go back and do it again. Musah is the most beloved of all Pharaoh's men. Almost all of them could name a time when Musah came through for them in some unforgettable way. Musah's heart is as big as he is and no one in Pharaoh's ranks would dare speak against him.

Pharaoh kneels beside the cot where Musah lays. Pharaoh studies his friend's face, then drops his eyes. He knows it's bad– *very bad*. Musah looks like a dead man. He is an ashen gray color and his eyes are glazed over. He is unresponsive, in a catatonic state of shock. His breathing is fast and shallow and beads of sweat cover his face. Pharaoh places his hand to Musah's forehead. He skin is ice cold.

"I have to be frank with you Pharaoh," the short, thin-framed, dark-skinned man begins. "It's not looking good for Musah." The doctor washes blood from his hands in a basin beside the cot. "The bullet pierced him in the side. His size worked to an advantage because it lodged in some bone and muscle tissue before reaching his heart. However, between the damage from the bullet and the broken ribs, one of two things will happen: either he will bleed out from the trauma or be poisoned to death by bone marrow." The doctor speaks quickly and competently to Pharaoh. "I have clamped off as many of the veins leading from his heart as I can to slow the bleed, but that's just a temporary fix for a very devastating condition. I don't want to remove the bullet without the resources that I need to repair the damage."

Pharaoh watches the doctor closely, dreading the words that he knows will come next.

"Pharaoh," Seneh sighs, wiping sweat from his lip and returning his glasses to his face. "There is a chance that Musah could pull through, but he needs surgery. I don't have the equipment or enough trained hands to help him. He must go to the nearest hospital now."

"**No**," Pharaoh roars. "Absolutely not!" He slices the air with his hand.

"He will die... very soon," the doctor pleads, softly challenging Pharaoh's decision. "There is nothing else I can do to stop it. Without surgery, he won't survive another hour."

"If he goes to the hospital with a gunshot wound, the police can link me and my organization back to ten dead bodies in an alley on Broadway." Pharaoh holds up his hands, displaying his ten fingers to illustrate the gravity of the situation.

All of the men in the room are tense. They don't want Musah to die but they can see the dilemma that Pharaoh faces as well.

"Look," Seneh begins strategizing a plan. "I will call ahead to the hospital and have Musah admitted as my patient, under an alias name."

Pharaoh's eyes become keen. He spins the plan around in his head, but finds a snag in it.

"How will you explain the gunshot wound?"

The doctor ponders, and then snaps his fingers. "Self-inflicted."

"Who shoots themselves in the ribs?" Pharaoh pulls the plan apart. "Musah is right-handed. The angle of entry would be virtually impossible for him."

All of the men go back to brainstorming, as Musah's breathing quickens, the short gasps so faint that they are barely audible.

"What about a robbery? We could say that he was attacked by an unknown assailant," Benny blurts enthusiastically, grateful to finally be able to help his friend.

Pharaoh wrinkles his brow with concentration, then releases it. "I'll take it." Pharaoh points at him, thanking Benny inaudibly with his eyes. "Rush Musah to the hospital," Pharaoh commands the men.

Benny, Jinx, Blaze and Action lift Musah off the cot. He is too weak to wince while the powerful men strain to carry him up the stairs.

"I will do my best to make sure that none of this can be traced back to you or the Golden Sphinx organization," the doctor assures Pharaoh; communicating an unspoken trust with his eyes. As the doctor starts the leave, he pats Pharaoh's shoulder lightly. Pharaoh struggles unsuccessfully to control the growl that escapes from his mouth. An intense, fiery pain shoots through his right arm. Pharaoh clutches his shoulder tightly, amazed by the powerful resurgence of the burning sensation that he has ignored for hours.

"Not you, too." Seneh's eyes are full of concern as he pulls off Pharaoh's suit jacket. Pharaoh tries to resist the small man, but his right arm is no longer cooperating with his will. The doctor presses Pharaoh down onto a low stool by the basement door. The doctor removes his shirt to find a large bloody gauze bandage wrapped around Pharaoh's shoulder.

"I guess you weren't going to mention this."

"Mention what?" Pharaoh winces while the doctor pulls the last of the gauze which has stuck to his skin.

"You could lose the use of this arm, if you don't let me get this bullet out." The doctor surveys the gaping hole. "You still might. There is some extensive damage here."

"Pharaoh will neither lose, nor give up anything," he issues boldly with a dismissive flip of his left hand.

"I'm going to phone the hospital so they will be ready for Musah, then I will work on that arm."

The doctor calls the hospital from a phone in Pharaoh's office at the far end of the basement and then returns shortly. He opens his huge medical bag and lays out a few instruments on a metallic tray. He places the tray on a small end table and begins his craft. The doctor offers to anesthetize the area before he begins, but Pharaoh refuses. He would rather get it over with. Every minute that passes now is costly to him.

Pharaoh bites down on his knuckles and utters a tiny grunt when the doctor digs into the wound. Within a few minutes, the doctor holds the gooey bullet within his large tweezers. A few minutes more and Seneh makes his best effort to stitch up the torn muscles and ligaments in Pharaoh's shoulder.

"Alright, Pharaoh. There's no damage to the bones, which is a good sign, but all the same you will have to keep this arm immobile for a few weeks to ensure that you don't tear apart all the work I just did." The doctor pulls a large, black sling out of his bag.

"No, Seneh." Pharaoh wags his finger. "I don't want the villains who did this to know they got a piece of me. They need to know that I cannot be touched."

"Pharaoh, if you don't listen to me, your adversaries are going to get more than just a piece of you. They are going to get a whole limb, because this arm won't be good for anything other than hanging expensive jackets on. I know you can't possibly want that."

Seneh forces Pharaoh, slipping his arm into the sling and adjusting the strap around his neck. He fastens a second strap around his back and tightens it to keep the arm stationary and pressed firmly against Pharaoh's stomach. Pharaoh looks with dismay at his reflection in the full-length, gold framed mirror on the wall beside the end table.

"If I have to wear this, do you think you could get me a gold one to match my bracelets?" He asks genuinely.

The doctor shakes his head and laughs lightly, as he rolls down his shirt sleeves. "Take these antibiotics." Seneh hands Pharaoh a small brown bottle. "I will keep you posted on Musah's condition, once he comes out of surgery."

Pharaoh nods his appreciation.

"Hey Boss, it's Blaze," he identifies himself at the door and Pharaoh opens it for him. "Everyone is here except for Sampson and Khassan, but they on the way."

"Go on and call everyone down," Pharaoh says, draping his jacket around his shoulders. Pharaoh would never admit this, but he is self-conscious about being wounded in front of his men. It puts a chink in his god armor. Most of them have never seen him have a cold or even be tired, let alone- injured.

The men file down into the basement. Jinx and Benny went to the hospital with Musah; but the other lieutenants, Action, Blaze and Johnny stayed behind. As senior-ranking officers, they know they need to be on hand for Pharaoh's business meeting. Also present are Pharaoh's trusted soldiers, Action's brother- Chaos,

Mannaseh, Jeepers, Donovan, Deitricks, Mayhem and Rufus.

The men sit on the edge of their seats, some on the sofa and others on aluminum folding chairs. Pharaoh stands beside his gold frame, high-back throne with red velvet cushions. Pharaoh still appears poised and regal with his shoulders squared and his eyes sharp before his men. As intimidating and awe-inspiring as Pharaoh's presence is, he lets his men be the eyes and ears of his organization. He shows his trust and dedication to them by allowing each of them to be a leader, second only to his command. Pharaoh lifts his left arm and extends his pointer finger to Blaze who stands in the corner behind the other men. All eyes in the room turn to him.

"This was an inside job," Blaze says lowly in a cryptic tone. He rubs his finger across his thick top lip. "This attack was very personal."

"But that's what I don't understand," Deitricks barges in. "What would make the Brothers come after you, Pharaoh? Everybody knows how you look after the ghetto."

"You think Long Beach was behind this?" Mannaseh asks quietly, turning his eyes to Pharaoh.

"I know it was Long Beach." Pharaoh joins the discussion. "One of those gunmen approached me a few weeks back when I was there. He told me he wanted to join Golden Sphinx. I told him that it didn't work that way. No one gets in and no one gets out. I told him that we don't recruit no new blood."

"That still doesn't answer the question," Blaze cuts in. "Why would Long Beach come after you, Pharaoh? You've showed nothing but love to the Brothers. Your money supports the entire community. They asses would be in the damn Dark Ages, nothing more than a Niggah Zoo, without you looking out for them."

"I think you just answered your own question, Blaze," Pharaoh remarks astutely. The men begin to nod in agreement.

"While the execution was Long Beach, I don't think they were the authors of this plot. They know better than to come for me like that. I think something provoked them. Something or someone made Long Beach jump ship."

"I put my money on them sneaky ass Italians," Mayhem blurts out. "They the only ones in LA that's got an axe to grind with you, Pharaoh."

Pharaoh turns it around his head. The wheels are spinning. He thinks they are on to something.

"It would be just like Piscitelli to start something cowardly like this," Johnny chimes in. "The least he could have done was face you his self."

"Action, the Italians are your section." Pharaoh turns his palm up, then places a finger to his chin. "What's the word on the streets?"

"Well... um," Action begins with some apprehension, choosing his words like a senior officer in Pharaoh's organization is trained to. Action knows, just as Musah, Benny, Blaze, Jinx and Johnny do, that Pharaoh does not want to hear their opinions or speculations. He wants competent, factual reports and clear, concise conclusions that can be supported with sound evidence. These six men are Pharaoh's lieutenants and therefore privileged to a deeper level of communion with him than the others. In all, there are only fifteen men in Pharaoh's organization as opposed to the hundreds that are in some of the rival enterprises, but this is more their strength than a weakness. Everyone in Pharaoh's organization is very well taken care of. They don't have to worry about splitting profits with an ever-growing number of runts and fledglings vying from within to attain position and status. These men are in the same ranks that they assumed in the Armed Forces. Pharaoh has always led them, as their Staff Sergeant before and as their King now. He never let any of them die in a god-forsaken, Charlie-infested rice paddy in Nam, so they trust him with their lives. It is their intelligence that got all of them back home- then and now. They have confidence in their ability to outwit LA's gangster hoodlums without having to outnumber them.

"Well," Action begins again, sucking his teeth as he pulls a toothpick out of his mouth. "It's like I told you last week, how Piscittelli's boys was shaking me down; telling me they needed a meeting with you 'cause they heard you was cutting the Brothers a break. I told them that they wasn't getting no meeting with you 'cause there wasn't nothing to discuss. I let 'em know that the Golden Sphinx's cut is the same no matter who's slicing the pie and they had been misinformed.

Pharaoh's gaze intensifies as he watches Action. Action smacks his fist against his palm. "I told them if they had a problem with our rates to take they business elsewhere, but after that everything cooled off. I ain't heard nothing else from the Italian camp since then."

"They could have easily done with that what they do with they product," Chaos adds sarcastically, popping the collar on his heavy, brown leather jacket. "Chopped up the story, watered it down, added some bullshit, and then sold it to the Brothers."

"That do make sense." Blaze points his finger with the realization. "The Italians probably told the Brothers you was cutting them the break. Maybe that's why that brother in Long Beach approached you. Maybe he was a Narc niggah that was going to report back and see if you was dealing fair between the two. But when they couldn't get in, they just decided to try and burn us down instead."

Pharaoh rubs his head, looking almost overwhelmed by the situation. He sighs heavily and rolls his neck to release some tension.

"Okay, we put the assassination attempt by the Brothers down. We got the who, the how and the why. Now what we don't have is a solution. This silly, disorganized, ill-prepared attack from the Brothers is bad for business. We have a lot of legitimate business holdings. This whole hustle revolves around those shares. If the square companies smell a rat then we won't have any place to wash our dirty laundry, gentlemen," Pharaoh states matter-of-factly. "But on the other hand, if we let this offensive go unpunished, then we will lose our reputation and we may end up paying for being on top so long with our lives."

"Are you talking retaliation, Pharaoh?" Chaos smiles, racking the slide on his Smith and Wesson. "Cause you know that's my specialty."

"What do you say, Donovan?" Pharaoh asks quietly.

Everyone's attention in the room turns to the intense, dark-skinned young man with the baldhead. Donovan rarely ever speaks but when he does his words are solid– well thought out. He is a deep, conscious brother and Pharaoh is secretly impressed with him. From his neat, well-tailored clothes to his stone-cold, poker face; Pharaoh sees his own image, like a mirror's reflection, in Donovan. Pharaoh is testing him. Pharaoh already has a plan in mind but he wants to see if Donovan has learned from him, if Donovan will say what he would say. Pharaoh wants to know if Donovan is in perfect fellowship with him. Donovan is his favorite disciple.

"Well-" Donovan begins assuredly. His deep voice is husky from lack of use. He is unpretentious but confidant when he speaks. "I say we hit the Brothers where it hurts. Smart work, not hard work. Take the financing out of the hood. The money speaks louder to the Brothers than violence will. I give the hood two weeks... tops, maybe less, and those unprofessional, small-minded baboons will destroy each other. Clearing the way for Golden Sphinx to sweep back in and pick up where we left off, unchallenged for supremacy in the game."

Pharaoh smiles inside, as his eyes narrow on Donovan. So far he is tracking with Pharaoh, step for step. That is exactly what Pharaoh would propose.

"When is the part where we get to shoot some guns," Mayhem bursts in, pointing to the racks with shelves of artillery and weapons lining the west wall of the basement. "It's been a long time since we got to shoot the guns and them targets at the range are boring as hell."

"Yeah," Chaos adds. "Y'all left us out of the gun play tonight and that ain't fair. Just cause that's his name don't mean *Action* should get all the **action**."

The men begin to laugh, but when they see that Pharaoh is not joining in their reindeer games, the laughter dies down quickly.

"Go on, Donovan." Pharaoh encourages him. "Explain for the simple ones."

"We bring the fire power to the Italians. They are the ones who need to know that Golden Sphinx ain't just a bunch of suit-wearing, pretty boys-"

"Speak for yourself," Pharaoh interjects playfully while straightening his suit jacket. The men laugh lightly at the expense of their general.

"I agree whole-heartedly with Donovan. Let's pull the funding out of the ghetto. The community will suffer for a while but it's a short-term loss for a long-term gain. We need to get those small time hoodlums out anyway. They will do our dirty work for us. Once we're not their competition anymore, they will turn on each other. That's the nature of the beast. It'll be ghetto genocide. In the meantime, move in hard- but quiet on the Italians; straight stealth sniper mode. Take 'em out in the restaurants while they're eating dinner and while they're playing in the park with their children... Take 'em out while they're in bed sexing their women and while they kneel in the pews at church to pray. Steady hands, clean shots, in and out. I want ten Italians, one of theirs for each one of the ten Brothers we killed in the street tonight. I want ten days and ten plagues of sheer terror for the Italians. I want them to open the newspaper every day and see another one of their own found dead. I want to be a cloud over their heads by day and a pillar of fire by night. I want them to fear the Golden Sphinx all day long, never knowing who's next to die. They will learn the price of betrayal. For stabbing Pharaoh in the back, they will be stabbed repeatedly in theirs. Because of them ten Brothers are dead and they almost killed one of our own, behind some bogus jive. This means war. Let's make the streets run red with Italian blood like a river. Is everybody with me?"

There is a consensus of nods in the room, but nothing is official in Golden Sphinx without a vote.

"All in favor," Pharaoh says, raising his left hand. All of the other hands follow likewise. Mayhem shoots his arm into the air, waving his hand like an eager child.

"Any opposed?" All of the hands drop. Pharaoh glances around the room to see that there is no opposition to the proposed course of action.

"Action and Blaze." Pharaoh points them out. "You coordinate the troops and report back. Donovan and Rufus, I have a special project for you two. I will meet with you separately after I handle some other business."

They nod and move in straightaway to begin delegating tasks. Action and Blaze divide the men into teams of two– a surveiller and a shooter. In each team, one man will be responsible for learning the routine of the target and finding the vulnerability in their defenses. The other team member will be responsible for taking the shot.

That is the greatest strength of Golden Sphinx: loyalty and organization. Pharaoh prepares to leave the basement, knowing that his men are capable of formulating an airtight military attack plan. Pharaoh ascends the stairs from the basement and emerges from the coat closet on the first level of the house. He slowly climbs the stairs to the second floor.

This house has been mostly empty for the last couple of years. With the exception of the occasional urgent business meeting, Pharaoh barely ever steps foot inside of it.

No one has really lived here since I died.

Pharaoh bought this house for me. We were going to start a family here. As volatile as our relationship was, I know he loved me. He didn't love me as much as he loves Cher but that's just because he was too young to appreciate what we had. Pharaoh's ability to love matures as he ages. What he put me through has taught him a little more temperance and now he can offer a fuller love to her than the wild, violent passion that we shared in our youth. Pharaoh stayed on in this house for a few months, but once I was gone, loneliness consumed him. The grief drove him back to the noise and distractions of the city, back to his bachelor pad.

Being in this house always makes Pharaoh think back to the good times we shared here. He smiles to himself, for just a moment, when he thinks of my happy laughter and loud singing drifting through the large rooms of the house. Pharaoh sees my smiling face beside his in the gold, as he brushes his hand along the railing. Pharaoh's nostalgia fades when he hears Cher moving around in the bedroom at the top of the stairs. Pharaoh feels a faint guilt wash over him for bringing her here, but then he dismisses it. This house was made for his family and Cher is his family now.

Pharaoh's housekeeper, Zipporah, cleans and dusts every week, whether anyone comes or not. Pharaoh likes the house to stay perfectly immaculate. He inspects the smudges on the gold railings. All of the fingerprints are slender and female, no doubt they belong to Cher. Pharaoh checks diligently to ensure that there are no other prints on the rails other than hers. Pharaoh trusts his men, but he has been betrayed before. Satisfied with his findings, he creeps into the master bedroom.

Pharaoh follows the glow of the candles to the large bathroom at the back of the suite. When Pharaoh sees Cher's long, silky leg hanging over the edge of the four-legged, porcelain tub, he almost forgets about all the crazy events of the night. The throbbing pain in his shoulder dissipates; just from the sight of her relaxing in a tub full of steaming, soapy water. Pharaoh watches a bead of sweat roll down her neck and over her breast. Cher breathes deeply and slowly. Pharaoh figures that she has slipped off to sleep under the folded washcloth that covers her eyes. Pharaoh sits on the edge of the tub and Cher doesn't even stir. He lightly brushes his lips on hers, startling her awake. Cher jumps slightly and pulls the washcloth from her face.

"Hey Papa." Her eyes soften immediately when they meet his. "I'm so glad to see you. I was worried." She rubs her hand along his neck. Cher can't help but be concerned for him, when she sees his arm in the sling.

"I told you that you never have to worry about anything, so long as you are with me." He runs his finger along the bridge of her nose. "I will always be with you. We are one now, remember?"

Cher nods. His presence is so overpowering that she shies in front of him. He is fresh out of battle and Cher can feel the strength of his command in her spirit.

"I know you must be tired," he remarks, gazing into her

drooping eyes. "A lot has happened tonight. You need to get some sleep before the sun comes up."

"I couldn't rest until I saw you... until I knew you were alright." Cher sighs wearily, rising from the bathtub. Pharaoh blows out the candles and reaches her a towel. Not having the use of his right arm hasn't bothered him more than at this moment. He wants to wrap Cher up in the towel and carry her exhausted body to his huge, round bed... but he can't... and that defeats the god in him. He can't even hold her hand because she would have to walk on his left side, so he just escorts her from the bathroom to the bed. Cher turns on a dim lamp and slips into Pharaoh's robe, which is laid across the armchair. She drops down on the edge of the soft bed and leans her head against Pharaoh's stomach. He gently strokes her hair. He is so glad that she didn't get hurt. He would have never forgiven himself, if she had. Cher is like a child before him. She trusts so completely in him. Pharaoh can feel how much she needs him to love and protect her. The god in him is uplifted by her faith.

"Goddess," he whispers so affectionately that Cher swoons for him when she peers up into his eyes. "I have to go away for a little while- just a few days. But I want you to stay here instead of at the penthouse."

A deep frown appears on Cher's face. She has not spent even one full day apart from Pharaoh since she came to LA and after tonight she didn't want to be separated from him for even one second. His cunning saved their lives and she couldn't feel safe without him.

"I will only be gone for a couple days, goddess. I promise." Pharaoh vows solemnly, gently caressing her chin. "Things are different now- and different times call for different measures, so I am going to do something that I have never done before. I have shown you that you can trust me with your life and now I have to know that I can trust you too."

"You can trust me with anything, Papa," she says, hugging his waist tightly.

"I have to go, but I would never leave you unprotected. I couldn't bear it if anything happened to you; so I am stationing Donovan and Rufus here at the house. I would rather leave Benny or Blaze, but I need all of my lieutenants with me, especially with Musah out of action."

Pharaoh shakes his head at the thought of his friend, then his mind steadies back on the instructions he has for Cher.

"I have never left any man in my crib with my woman. To be alone with my goddess is an honor that I reserve only for myself; but under the circumstances, I have no other alternative. I want you safe, so I am leaving Donovan, my best brain and Rufus, my best gun here with you."

Cher can tell that Pharaoh is apprehensive about the decision, but she doesn't understand why. No man has ever made her feel the way Pharaoh does. He should know that he doesn't have to worry about another man, and especially not one of his own, when it comes to her.

Cher stands from the bed and wraps her arms around his neck. "Papa, I would **never** betray you," she issues intensely, assuring him with the passion in her eyes. "I love you."

"I love you too, goddess." He kisses her lips, clutching the back of her head tightly.

An intercom speaker by the bedroom door buzzes. Pharaoh walks over and depresses the button.

"Yeah," he speaks into the box.

"Sampson and Khassan are here. They need to talk to you."

"Be right down," Pharaoh answers shortly. He steps back over to Cher. "Duty calls, sweetheart. My men and I are about to leave. Donovan and Rufus are going to stay, so you just rest now.

Everything will be alright. My housekeeper, Zipporah, will be here later this morning with some of your things from the penthouse and she will take care of you. Just relax and pretend it is a vacation. Okay?"

"Okay." Cher nods her compliance. She doesn't want Pharaoh to know how afraid she is for him to leave her. Pharaoh pulls back the soft, gold-colored jersey sheets and motions with his head for Cher to lie down. Once she is lying comfortably, he tucks the duvet under her chin and presses his lips to her forehead. Pharaoh clicks off the bedside lamp and heads for the door. Pharaoh slips from the room, taking all of the light that spilled in from the hallway with him. Within seconds of the darkness closing in on her, Cher is fast asleep.

Pharaoh trots down the stairs and is met by Sampson on the bottom step. Sampson is a large, muscular caramel-complexion man; a certifiable giant towering a few inches even over Pharaoh. He has long, soft cornrows and a tiny, gold hoop in each of his ears.

"We was on our way here, when we got caught up in Long Beach," he says, his voice little more than a rumbling vibration. "Some hoodlums tried to rob Big Mama tonight."

"**What**?" Pharaoh bellows. "Who was on patrol in Long Beach?"

"I was," Khassan answers nervously. "But they told me you was pulling everybody, so I went to get Sampson. We were on our way up here when Sharessa stepped out in the street to stop our car."

Pharaoh breathes heavily; his eyes full of rage.

"You can't blame him, Pharaoh. There was so much shit going on in Long Beach tonight ain't no way he could have been everywhere all at one time. Word got out down there that the

Brothers killed you. The whole place went wild."

"The Brothers went after Big Mama too?" Blaze asks cautiously, not sure if he is allowed in the conversation.

"Oh hell, no. the Brothers know better. No one would respect they asses if they did some shit like that," Sampson growls. "This was some ignorant ass teenagers from another block who didn't know who she was. They probably figured she was some helpless old lady they could knock over for a few valuables."

"Sharessa says that Big Mama's next door neighbor, Juney, heard the boys kick her door in, so he called the police and went to help. She said by the time the police got there the whole neighborhood was in Big Mama's front yard whooping them kids' asses." Khassan recounts with a serious expression.

"The cops got them. So, I'm pretty sure when the Brothers in lock up find out what them boys in there for, they probably gone fuck 'em up real good." Sampson replies with subdued satisfaction.

"The Brothers in Long Beach still swearing they allegiance to you, Pharaoh. They say them renegade niggahs that attacked you didn't have nothing to do with them," Khassan adds soberly.

"Where's Big Mama now?" Pharaoh asks calmly.

"She's in the hospital. The scare was too much for her heart." Sampson drops his eyes.

"Take me there now," Pharaoh commands, already heading for the door.

# GRANDMA'S HANDS

When Pharaoh arrives at the hospital, Big Mama is hooked up to several machines. She has an oxygen mask on her face, taking deep, slow breaths. She doesn't seem to be in any pain, just resting in her hospital bed. Pharaoh touches her soft, wrinkled hand and her left eye opens. The other eye is not so cooperative, peeking only a tiny bit to look at him. A small grin appears on her lips to see him. Pharaoh's eyes sting and moisten as he looks at his Big Mama. He loves her so much. It is breaking his heart to see her this way.

"I'm going to get you the best doctors and heart specialists that money can buy. I can't lose you Big Mama."

She pats his hand and gazes lovingly into his eyes. Big Mama reaches up to pull her mask down.

"No Big Mama," Pharaoh says, reaching for her hand. Big Mama pops the back of his hand and takes off the oxygen.

"Sugar, don't waste your time on this old woman," she huffs in a thin, faint voice. "I'm on my way up yonder to be with my Lord."

"Don't talk like that. You still got a lot left to do. I need you here with me." Pharaoh kisses her cheek. Pharaoh keeps his jacket closed tightly, shielding his right side. He doesn't want her to see his arm in the sling.

"Bless your heart, Mason," she sighs, rubbing his cheek. "But baby, this ain't up to you. Your Big Mama is ti'ed. She done fought hard in this battle and she is ready to be released from service." She offers Pharaoh a sincere, toothless grin. "I been so lonely all these years. I miss my husband, Albert, and now I'm finally gone get to see him again."

Pharaoh tries his best to be strong, to be the rock for his Big Mama, but he can't. She has always been the rock for him. The thought of losing her overwhelms him and he begins to cry, breaking down into sobs on his grandmother's shoulder.

"Shhh," she hisses forcefully, patting his trembling back. "Don't you cry for me, Sugar. I'm going to a better place than the one you planned for me in Beverly Hills. You won't have to worry about me *no more*." She stresses the words. "I'll be safe and happy now."

"But I'm gone miss you, Big Mama. You all the flesh and blood that I got." He places the soft, wrinkled flesh of her slender hand on his cheek.

"And we gone *always* be flesh and blood, Mason. Death can't change that. You gone have my love with you as long as you live. I'm gone be right here in your heart. Every time it beat, my blood gone flow through your veins. You ain't gone never be rid of me." She taps his shoulder playfully. "I only waited here to tell you goodbye. I love you, Mason."
She squeezes his hand, as a tear rolls down her face.

"l love you too, Big Mama," Pharaoh issues in hiccups between his sobs, wiping his eyes with the back of his hand.

Big Mama breathes in deeply. The breath struggles in her chest. Then just as quickly as she drew the breath in, she exhales and her body gives up the ghost. In unison, the alarms and sirens on the machines begin to sound. Pharaoh cannot endure the blare of them. They impede his ability to make peace with what has just happened. Suddenly, his rage burst free from him and he pulls the machines down in frustration.

The nurses rush into the room to find him destroying the equipment. They disregard him for the moment and attempt to resuscitate his grandmother, but Pharaoh stands and raises his voice.

"Leave her alone! Just let her go. That's what she wants, so give her whatever she wants," he pants dejectedly and then walks out of the room.

Time stands still for Pharaoh, as he walks down the corridor to the exit of the hospital. He feels like he is passing the rooms in slow motion. A couple of nurses step into his path to ask if they can assist, but he waves them off and continues down what seems like a mile-long hallway- a corridor to forever.

He runs his hands through his hair and tries to clear his head and heart of all the conflicting emotions. He has to be strong. Big Mama is gone now and being sad about it isn't going to bring her back. She was right about one thing- her departure meant one less person he had to protect. Pharaoh still has the safety of his empire, his woman and his men to think about. His mind is like a stormy sea and his thoughts are sharks, each one devouring the other. By the time Pharaoh finally reaches the car and slinks into the backseat, he is too confused and distraught to talk.

So when Sampson asks, "How is Big Mama?" The look on Pharaoh's face is enough for him to turn back around in the driver's seat and drive away silently.

# THE CLEAN-UP WOMAN

Four days passed before Cher saw Pharaoh again.

Four long... slow... uneventful days.

During the four days, she didn't hear from Pharaoh even once. Zipporah showed up at the house in the early afternoon of the first day. She came bearing many of Cher's personal belongings. She packed Cher up like she was never going back to the penthouse. Almost everything Cher owned was in the trunk of the Rolls Royce when Zipporah pulled up with Jinx and Benny. The men helped unpack the car, but only the women lugged the suitcases, coats and make-up kits up the stairs to the bedroom.

Cher didn't know until Benny and Jinx left the bags on the foyer floor and then went into the kitchen with Donovan and Rufus, that the men weren't allowed upstairs. But they sure knew and didn't seem at all obliged to help the women as they heaved and strained against the weight of the bags. They continued their impromptu, informal meeting with hushed voices and without so much as a glance in the direction of the females.

Cher realized quickly that Pharaoh has a method for everything. Cher didn't really need two bodyguards. They were locked up inside the almost air-tight security of the estate, but Donovan and Rufus were a cover for each other. If either one of them tried something out of the way with Cher, then the other would definitely tell Pharaoh. The two of them were like Siamese twins, rarely out of each other's sight. They did almost everything, except go to the bathroom and shower, together. They were each other's alibi more than anything else. Zipporah, however, was Cher's shadow. She discovered early on that Zipporah's capacity was more than just domestic. She seemed to pay more attention to Cher than any other activity in the house. She waited outside of the bathroom when Cher showered, offering to lay out her clothes. She invited Cher into the kitchen to help with the cooking, as if she really needed any.

Zipporah delivered the meals to the men in the guesthouse, and then she would dine daily with Cher in the main house. Other than the occasional visit from one of Pharaoh's lieutenants for Rufus and Donovan, the routine remained the same each day.

The first evening that Cher dined with Zipporah, she took her time to take the woman all in. Zipporah was, no doubt, a spy for Pharaoh. She was courteous and made polite small talk with Cher, but the way Zipporah stalked her all over the house gave away her secret assignment. Zipporah was going over the top and way beyond the call of duty to do surveillance on her which let Cher know that she was looking for a way to usurp her. She was searching for any speck of dirt to expose to Pharaoh.

Zipporah is pretty foxy- like *gorgeous*, to be a housekeeper. Most maids are frumpy, homely-looking creatures, but not Zipporah. She makes her modest gray uniform dress and white apron look like it is being worn by a Playboy Bunny. She is tall, and young, maybe twenty-seven, give or take a couple of years. She wears her hair cut in a short, sleek bob that contours her sharp, jaw line. Zipporah has a smooth, almond complexion and large, slanted hazel eyes. Between her full lips and hips, she is almost– but not quite, the knockout that Cher is. Cher didn't feel threatened by her at first, but after the first couple days, she realized that maybe she should.

A woman can tell when another woman has laid with her man. Something about the energy between them didn't feel quite right to Cher. It was off-balance. Zipporah was subdued and submissive towards her, offering to help and doing whatever she was told. But something in the way she looked at Cher and strutted around in her presence let her know that Zipporah was sizing her up, wondering what Cher had that she didn't. Zipporah was so taken with Pharaoh that she couldn't hide her true feelings and intentions from Cher. It was written all over Zipporah, from her face down to her pigeon-toed feet, that she had tasted Pharaoh's cup and wanted desperately to drink from his fountain.

After Cher recognized that was probably the case, she didn't shy away from Zipporah, but began to stalk her back; making more requests than usual and doing her best to exasperate the woman. Cher might have been upset at the prospect of Zipporah bedding down her man, but instead she decided to show her who the Boss Bitch is in the house. Cher figured that Zipporah couldn't have been getting any more action from Pharaoh, since she started taking up all of his free time.

Unless Pharaoh is as superhuman as he claims to be, there would be no way that he could give it to her as often as he has and still have any energy left over for Zipporah. Cher knew enough about females anyway to know that if Zipporah did have anything solid going with Pharaoh, she wouldn't be working so hard to get her out of the picture. Their relationship had reached full-fledged arch rivalry by the time Pharaoh returned to the house.

"I want her out of here **now**," are Cher's first words to Pharaoh when he comes through the door.

"What's going on?" Pharaoh asks with an extended hand, waiting to embrace his woman. Instead, Cher stands tapping her foot with crossed arms. "What's got you so bent out of shape, goddess?"

"Zipporah has got to go. I don't want her here anymore."

Zipporah breezes quietly into the foyer and helps Pharaoh's out of his coat. Cher eyes her suspiciously, wanting to yank her hair out, when she touches him and takes his coat to the closet.

"Did something happen?... Did she do something wrong?" Pharaoh's eyes dart between both women.

"No," Cher answers shortly, rolling her eyes. Zipporah

likewise lowers her eyes and shakes her head, communicating nonverbally to Pharaoh not only her own innocence, but Cher's as well.

"Alright," he sighs with a tone of resignation. "Zipporah, I will send you your things from the house and give you a good reference with two weeks' severance pay, but today is your last day."

Zipporah's eyes blaze with rage when she cuts them at Cher. Cher gloats internally, letting the satisfaction show on her face.

"But, Pharaoh," she pleads. "Miss Cher just said that I didn't do anything wrong."

"If the goddess is not pleased with you for whatever reason, then you must go." Pharaoh shrugs his shoulders. "I will have Benny take you home now."

"But Pharaoh," she begs, gripping his shirt.

Pharaoh becomes angered at her touching him and pulls her hands away. "Be still, woman. Don't make me tell you again, Zipporah," he threatens through tightened lips.

A tear drops from Zipporah's eye, as she obediently backs away from him. She swallows hard and gets her coat from the closet. She shoots Cher, who is already hugging Pharaoh and pecking tiny kisses on his lips, a dirty look before she throws open the door. Benny is outside helping Musah up the front steps when Zipporah steps onto the porch.

"Benny, I need you to take Zipporah home, please." Pharaoh calls to him mildly, still staring into Cher's eyes. Pharaoh missed her so much that the sight of her captures all of his focus.

Zipporah leaves the door open and greets Musah when she passes him on the front steps. Under different circumstances, she would make conversation, but she is so heartbroken that she just slips into the back seat of the Monte Carlo and waits for Benny to return.

"Cher," Pharaoh begins. "Musah will be staying with us in the guesthouse, until he gets a little stronger."

Musah looks pretty well, when he steps through the door. Considering his condition the last time Cher saw him, it could almost be considered a tiny miracle. Maybe Pharaoh and his men are invincible after all. Cher is glad to see him doing so well, but she doesn't want to show it on her face in front of Pharaoh.

"Glad you're better, Musah." Cher says in an even, diplomatic tone.

And for the first time, Musah acknowledges something other than a request from her.

"Thank you," he says graciously, offering a polite smile with no eye contact. Musah's eyes go instead to Pharaoh, as if the gratitude for Cher's comment belongs to him.

"Okay, goddess. Let me get Musah settled in out back. The doctors say he needs lots and lots of rest." Pharaoh pats his shoulder genially.

Benny leaves out of the front door while Pharaoh and Musah move slowly through the kitchen to the back door.

Soon all of the movement around the estate is finished and everyone settles down. Donovan and Rufus are relieved of duty and Musah takes their place in the guesthouse. Before, they leave the estate with Benny and Zipporah, Pharaoh brings his belongings in from the car and up to the master bedroom. Cher can see, as he unpacks, that there stay in Echo Park isn't going to be a short one.

Later in the afternoon, Pharaoh comes to Cher.

"Goddess, can you prepare dinner? I will begin looking for Zipporah's replacement in the morning, but for now-"

"Say no more, my King." Cher rises gracefully from the sofa. "I can handle that, Papa."

"Thank you, Love." Pharaoh kisses her cheek before she leaves the living room.

A few somewhat complicated hours later, Cher manages to create a decent meal of baked chicken legs, red beans with rice, collards and corn bread for them. The hardest part of preparing dinner was finding all the ingredients. The huge pantry at the front of the kitchen seems like it is fortified for nuclear fallout. It is more like a giant storehouse of its own, stocked from floor to ceiling with shelves of dry and canned goods. It is expansive and organized in some weird, catalogued system that only its author, no doubt Zipporah, would understand.

Cher alerts Pharaoh, who is napping upstairs in the bedroom, over the intercom that dinner is ready. She fixes a plate for Musah, but unsure of what to do with it, she leaves it on the counter and set places for her and Pharaoh at the dinner table.

"Mmm," Pharaoh says, sniffing deeply when he walks into the kitchen. "Smells good, goddess."

He walks up behind her and encircles her waist with his arms. He pulls her tightly to him and kisses her neck. Cher's body ignites with passion for him. During his absence, she missed Pharaoh so much. She was about to ask him, if they could push dinner back for a little reconnection time, but Pharaoh quickly extinguishes her heat when he asks if he can take his dinner in the guesthouse with Musah.

"Sure, Papa. Whatever you want," she answers dejectedly and helps Pharaoh to cover the plates with plastic wrap. He takes them both in his left hand and leaves out of the back door.

Cher is left to eat alone by candlelight in the dining room. She starts to think that if this is going to be the regular routine, then maybe Zipporah wasn't such a terrible dinner date after all.

# THE WORLD IS A GHETTO

Pharaoh leaves the main house, closing the back door on Cher, and crosses the grounds to the guesthouse. The two-bedroom guesthouse is an exquisite, scaled down replica of the main house with its own living room, kitchen with breakfast nook and large, full bath.

"Musah," Pharaoh begins cautiously, watching his friend across the table. "You know that there is no one in this organization that I trust more than you, or whose opinion matters more to me than yours-"

Musah sits bare-chest with a bandage wrapped around his torso. When they wheeled him into surgery almost five days ago, Musah was about as close to death as anyone could be and still survive. After a few blood transfusions and some extensive surgery to remove the bullet and repair the damage, Musah is almost as good as new, except for a few tender incisions under his left arm and on the left side of his chest. Just as Dr. Seneh promised, the medical chart and police report for *Mr. James Williamson* read that he was robbed at gunpoint by a Black man wearing a stocking over his face. The cops took the cover story, open-and-shut case. A Black-on-Black crime in the ghetto didn't warrant any further investigation.

When Musah was released from the hospital, Pharaoh brought him back to the house instead of taking him to his apartment. Pharaoh refused to let him go, despite his insistence that he didn't need a babysitter. Musah didn't know that Pharaoh needed him there, more than he needed to be there, until this conversation.

"You are my right hand." Pharaoh points to his arm in the sling. "I refuse to imagine the thought of losing you."

Pharaoh is rarely sentimental, so Musah knows how concerned he must have been.

"Pharaoh, you know I'm not going anywhere. I wouldn't bail on you, just like I didn't when Charlie surrounded us in Nam,"

Musah says confidently, taking a few bites from his plate.

"Look, I haven't talked to any of the other men about this. You're the only person that I want in on it," Pharaoh states in urgent breaths. His eyes dark and steady on Musah.

"Consider me your priest, Pharaoh, cause you know anything you tell me will be buried with me in my grave."

"I already brought you up to speed about the plan, but for the past few days, I have been doing the numbers. Now that we've pulled the money away from Long Beach and the Italians, I don't know if Golden Sphinx can survive the hit. I've tried to reinvest more funds into the legitimate financial services branch of our organization, but it doesn't yield the same return, maybe in the long run, but it was a poor short-term investment option. I wanted to believe that the company was solvent enough to stay afloat without Long Beach; but the truth is, we just might drown trying to sink them. If we go back to them first, then they will think we are weak and try to capitalize on our Achilles heel."

"Well Pharaoh if you want my honest opinion as your business partner, I would say it's about as good a time as ever to expand operations. I know how you feel about that because of how small our operation is, but we made some pretty solid contacts in Vegas. We will never know if that market is a viable option until we try it."

"If everyone we met in Vegas is as slimy and disrespectful as that damn Leroy then I don't want no part of Vegas."

A faint laugh of amusement escapes Musah's mouth, before the sharp pain pierces his side.

"Leroy wasn't that bad," Musah says playfully, turning up his palm. "He just didn't know you. He got caught up for a minute, but who could blame him for that."

The words slip out before Musah can think about them. He curses himself for being so careless. He doesn't have to look at

Pharaoh to know that he overstepped the boundary. Pharaoh's eyes lock on Musah, watching him like prey. Musah scoops a big bite of beans into his mouth.

"But that niggah don't matter no more anyway. His ass at the bottom of a cliff somewhere out in Death Valley." He tries to smooth things over with Pharaoh by reiterating to him that he knows the penalty for betrayal.

"Yeah," Pharaoh says with a smile on his lips, but coldness in his eyes. "That is very true."

Musah slices the silence.

"If you're asking my professional opinion, I think that's the best route to go right now. Vegas is a booming area with a lot more tourism than LA. That place is a gold mine, both for legitimate business ventures as well as hustling and we are just sitting on it." Musah jabs his fork in the chicken on his plate and turns the conversation back to the only thing Pharaoh loves more than his woman– his business.

"Alright, I'll put Blaze on the set up, since he's been itching to go out there- but are you sure?... I can't afford to station anyone so far away from headquarters with all the shit popping off here in LA. Do you think Vegas can run itself?"

Musah shrugs his shoulders. "Start off with a baby operation, just a few hungry newborns you can trust with small money, then if it goes well and we get this shit straight in LA, you can send one of the lieutenants to permanently oversee the operation."

"How will the others feel about that. We said no new blood."

"We also said that different times, call for different measures. Last time we took a vote on it, the men were almost half and half about taking in new members. Under these circumstances, they might finally be in favor of adding a few new faces. If not, then we can try a basic set up in Vegas and use whatever profits we can raise to help keep Golden Sphinx solvent while we regulate in LA, then bag the operation and put the money back into Long Beach."

Pharaoh nods confidently, but then hisses as he shakes his head. "I don't know," Pharaoh sighs cautiously.

"Look Vegas was pretty good for your love life. Maybe it can be just as good for business too." Musah offers Pharaoh a smile and he returns it slowly.

Musah was right. Pharaoh was beginning to think that Cher was a bit of a good luck charm for him. Before all of this madness broke out, business had never been better. Maybe it was the positive attitude that being in love revived in him, but he had more legitimate business investments than ever. White corporate businessmen were lining up to dip their hands into Pharaoh's pocket and pay him out handsomely for allowing them to do it.

Musah draws a line in the conversation. "But that's just my advice... as a business partner."

"Are you divided on the issue Musah?" Pharaoh asks perceptively.

"Can I tell you what I think as a friend?"

"Of course," he replies shortly, gesturing the go-ahead with his hand.

"As your friend, I think it's time to pack it up and get out of the game for good." Pharaoh lifts an eyebrow. This is something he never expected to hear Musah say. "Golden Sphinx Financial Firm has enough legitimate investments and shareholdings to thrive as a straight-up, square-ass company. We won't all be pushing boss rides and wearing tailor-made threads but we could learn to minimize and adapt to the change."

Pharaoh watches Musah closely and quietly. He figures that taking a bullet has stolen some of his vigor. His near death experience has him second-guessing his involvement in the business.

"Hear me out," he continues. "We been going non-stop, around the clock for almost seven years. We have built an unimaginable empire on the back of so few men that it would be impossible for anyone other than us to do it. I'm thirty-three, Pharaoh and I almost died on Broadway Street without anybody to cry for me. I don't have a woman because no decent one could tolerate my lifestyle and I would never put a baby into any one of them triflin' stellas I fuck with. It's time for a change, man. I know even you can see that 'cause you settling down and setting up house again with your female. Maybe if we all go legit, we can finally have a life outside of this business and feel safe starting our families without having to lock them up behind bars like prisoners. Then we can expand our operations and maybe even you can escape this city that has held you like a prisoner over the years too. Maybe then you can take a vacation, every now and then. Go and see the world, the pyramids even, with your woman."

"So you're talking about sitting behind desks, pushing paper around all day like bankers, right?"

"Yeah, something like that. We got a pretty good reputation in the corporate arena. It wouldn't be hard for us to make the switch. We started this organization with dirty money, but maybe we can finally wash our hands clean."

"Mmm hmmm," Pharaoh mumbles introspectively, stroking his chin. Musah smiles a bit, hoping that the potentate is considering his proposal, but Musah's smile fades when Pharaoh begins to speak because he knows instantly that wasn't the case.

"I'm sorry Musah but I can't do that. It's like you said, we built this company on certain principles. We were raised on these streets, raised on the hustle. It was those principles that made our venture a success. We went straight before, tried to make our families proud. We graduated and did the military gig, but what did that get us– hunh, Musah?... Spit on and hated in our own country- that's what. It was bad enough to be Black in America, but being Vietnam veterans made it double. We went over there in a savage jungle and almost gave our lives for a cause that didn't nobody even give a damn about. That war continued on for years even after we left it. This drug game is the same. Long after we gone, someone else will still be making money hand over fist. We've laid our lives on the line for way less than all this fabulous living we got going on right now. I say if there's still money to be made then we should be the ones to make it."

"But how do you sleep at night knowing that we doping up our own community– our own neighborhoods?"

"I sleep just fucking fine on soft satin sheets. That's how!" Pharaoh bellows, standing up from his seat. "You expect me to feel bad about this shit, Musah? If it wasn't us, then it would be the Italians and the Chinese drugging out the neighborhood and selling them a bullshit ass product without a conscious. We have put a lot of Black men to work. We have fed a lot of Black children. We have used the money from the community to take care of the poor and the elderly. It was money that Black mothers and Black fathers would not have spent to educate their Black children, or patronize their Black-owned businesses, or beautify their own Black neighborhoods, because they were too busy buying smack to shoot up in their veins. But we took their money... and we did with it what they wouldn't. We bought a beautiful, Black American dream with the money. We even used White money to take care of the ghetto and keep it from going to shit."

Musah can tell that Pharaoh is beside himself with anger, but not at him, just at the situation.

"I refuse to apologize, Musah. I didn't do this to our

community. I just profited from it, but when Pharaoh came up, we all came up. We all got a piece of a pie that wasn't made for us or by us, but I am just glad to be the one with the knife instead of the cops, or the Italians or the Chinese who would only use it to destroy the community completely."

Musah never knew that Pharaoh felt this way. He always knew that hustling was in his blood, but he didn't know how he bled for his community.

"You want to know what does keep me up at night? You want to know what nightmares make me wake up holding a gun to my own head?" Pharaoh's eyes darken. "Remember that night we had to set that house full of Vietnamese woman and children on fire because they told us they were hiding weapons for Charlie?... Do you remember that Musah?"

Musah swallows hard. His face loses it color and he looks faint. "Yeah," he whispers on a shaky breath. "I remember."

"That's the shit that bathes me in cold sweat at night. All those people we killed, just murdered them like dogs, and for what? At least here we got a reason to fight. At least here, in our own streets, we know who the real enemy is. I cannot leave the game, Musah. It's all I got. I am the game and the game is me. We are one in the same and we cannot be divided. I can't just fade into the background and be satisfied to walk down the street without people knowing my name. I've never lived that way and I won't start now. I can't just crawl away on my hands and knees like a coward, when Golden Sphinx takes a hit. I'll never let them think they were the ones to take us down. I won't just scurry away with my tail between my legs. It's more than the money- my reputation is on the line. I am god in LA, Musah. The only way I will ever go out in the game is on top." Pharaoh pats his chest.

"I would rather have died at the top of my game, alone on Broadway that night, than hand this game over to someone else.

That's the difference between you and me. You got nothing else to lose if you walk away now."

"Pharaoh, I wasn't talking about walking away from the organization. I was just talking about a different direction, but you the Boss Man. Whatever Pharaoh says is what goes."

"Look I swore an oath by myself that we all started together and we was all going to end this together. No one gets in and no one gets out, but different times call for different measures. If we can entertain the idea of adding bodies, then it's only fair that I let you go, Musah." Pharaoh states the words with sad finality.

"Nah, Pharaoh. I told you I don't want out."

"It's not your decision, Musah. I have heard your concern and I can't ignore that. I can't ask you to continue on this way when your heart ain't in the game no more. That could cost you your life the next time. I'd rather release you, than see that happen."

Musah stands slowly to protest. "Pharaoh, I-"

"Say no more, Musah. It is decided. You saved my life once and now I am going to give you back the life that you gave to me."

Pharaoh takes the dog tags that he has been wearing around his neck for seven years and gives them back to Musah.

"I'll have the lawyers draw it up tomorrow. You and your shares are leaving Golden Sphinx." Pharaoh presses the long, thin silver chain into his palm.

"Pharaoh, I can't take this money out of the company, when you need it and me the most. I just can't do that."

"You can't- but I can. We have come back from worse slumps than this before and we will do it again. The money wasn't ours anyway. It was always yours to do with it what you want. Maybe now you can set up house in Alabama, get married and start a construction company or a landscaping business, or whatever kind of square gig you want." Pharaoh smiles, patting Musah's shoulder.

Musah resigns. He knows he can't fight Pharaoh on this.

"I'ma miss you, man." Musah takes off the dog tags he has been wearing and gives them to Pharaoh. He wraps his massive arms around Pharaoh's lean torso. Both men are misty-eyed.

"And I, you, my friend and my most trusted lieutenant." Pharaoh returns his embrace, then takes a step back. "Just stay with me until after Big Mama's funeral and I'll let Benny go back to Alabama with you for a few days, just to help you get settled."

Pharaoh starts for the door, then stops abruptly as he turns the knob.

"Who knows, maybe I'll even come out there one day. I can be god in Birmingham, too." Pharaoh smiles before disappearing out of the door.

****

The house is dark when Pharaoh comes back inside. Cher is asleep on the bed, laying across the covers when Pharaoh creeps into the bedroom. It's still pretty early, so Pharaoh figures it was boredom more than fatigue that put her to sleep.

Pharaoh sits down in the armchair beside the bed. He watches her sleep for a few minutes, allowing her soft, feminine presence to bring balance to his spirit. He watches her breathe in deep and longs to be that breath, to be inside of her, and one with her. He brushes the foot that hangs off the bed to wake her.

"Hey, Papa," she sighs, staring at him from across the bed. Pharaoh is seduced and energized by her eyes on him. She watches his face as she slides off the edge of the bed and crawls over to him. She wraps her body around his leg and lays her head in his lap.

"I missed you so much, Papa." Her eyes are sad and sincere.

"Really?" Pharaoh asks with a surprised tone. Cher nods,

staring up at him like a child. Pharaoh leans down to kiss her forehead.

"I've missed you too, goddess." His hand is heavy on her head, as he smoothes her hair. "I've had a rough few days and I couldn't wait to get back here to you. I knew that seeing you would make it just a little easier."

Cher didn't want to ask, but she didn't want to seem like she didn't care either. The truth was that she desperately wanted to know what exactly was going on. She had been in the dark since the night of the shooting and had no idea what any of the events meant.

"Do you want to talk about it?" Cher asks with quiet cautiousness.

"Actually, I would love to discuss it with you... if you don't mind?"

"Go ahead and get it off your chest, Papa. I'm here for you."

Pharaoh sighs long, staring out through the sheer window coverings at the moon. "Big Mama died," he breathes with moist eyes.

Cher can feel the sting in her eyes when she sees the pain in his.

"I'm so sorry, baby," Cher says, taking the weight of his grief on her back and sharing the load with him.

"It's alright. Part of me is sad, but another bigger part of me is glad. She is resting now. I don't have to worry if she is safe, or warm, or eating right anymore. I know she is happy now. The funeral is tomorrow," he whispers passively.

A lone tear rolls from his eye. Cher reaches up and wipes it away with her thumb. She takes his hand and presses it to her lips.

"Musah is leaving as well. I'm sending him back to Alabama."

Cher is surprised to see that news seems to be more upsetting for Pharaoh than Big Mama's death.

"Wow, you *have* been through a lot over the past few days," Cher says sympathetically, rubbing his calf. "I wish there was something I could do."

"You have already done enough, Love. Just being a soft place for me to land means so much to me."

"Anything for my King," Cher replies genuinely. She is so in love with her man when he is this vulnerable with her. How can she not open her whole heart up to him? He needs the strength of her love to heal him now.

"Do you want to pick the new housekeeper, or do you want me to?" Pharaoh wipes his eyes and changes the subject. Cher follows his lead. She doesn't want to ruffle his feathers by pressing for more information.

"Well, I don't care either way. I only ask that if you pick, please don't let it be another woman that you have bedded down."

Pharaoh laughs lightly, then lifts Cher's chin with his finger. "Is that what you think happened between Zipporah and me?"

"I don't care what happened between you and Zipporah. I just don't want any competition in our home."

"There is no competition for you on this planet, filet. I told you already, you are one with me and no other female can have that place. I love you... and no one else. I have chosen only you to be my goddess. We have only one life between the two of us now. As long as I live, there can be no other woman for me– but you. Only death can separate us now."

Cher's loins throb with passion at his words. Cher's boils inside for Pharaoh. She wants him to take her, but he puts a lid on her instead.

"I have known Zipporah for a very long time, since we were

kids even. She grew up with me down in Long Beach. I heard around the neighborhood that she used to crush on me back in high school, but we are way past that now. I have always kept my business separate from my personal life and she knows that. She has worked for me for over five years, since I brought this house. She was here with me and Bel–" Pharaoh stops abruptly, like he has just seen a ghost.

"What's the matter?" Cher asks curiously.

"Nothing," Pharaoh says dismissively, trying to cool Cher's suspicion. "I just forgot to do something at my office, but it can wait until tomorrow."

"Well, rap on and finish what you were saying."

"I can't remember now," Pharaoh replies with a puzzled expression, like his mind has been wiped blank. "All I can tell you is that Zipporah has never felt Pharaoh's love inside of her. She has never experienced what I give only to the goddess." Pharaoh pulls Cher into his lap. "Maybe she longs to, but there are many women who share that fantasy with her and none of them will ever get the opportunity. Trust me. I would not have left you alone with her if I had slept with her. She would have murdered you in your sleep." Pharaoh laughs lightly.

Cher thought about it for a minute. Pharaoh did have a point. His love was to die for– maybe even to kill for. Cher would definitely consider it if Pharaoh ever left her for another woman. Maybe she was wrong about Zipporah after all.

"Did you have me fire her out of jealousy?'

Cher straddles his laps. She shrugs her shoulders and pouts her bottom lip.

"I can't believe that you're jealous of Zipporah." Pharaoh glares at Cher disapprovingly. "If you are going to get upset about every woman the desires your Pharaoh, then you plan on spending a lot of time angry. This is a trait most unbecoming of a goddess and very unprofessional. You must learn to keep your heart out of business affairs, honey." He kisses her neck. "Business should never be personal. If you are going to reign with me, you have to be able to keep them separate."

Pharaoh caresses her chin. "Pharaoh is loyal to his woman, his men, his business and his employees. I won't go against what my goddess desires, but I would ask that you reconsider your decision about Zipporah. She has a child and I do not want her to suffer behind your ignorance. I am swearing to you now that nothing has nor ever will happen between me and Zipporah. Take the light of that knowledge and search your heart. The final decision is yours."

"Okay," Cher drawls, knowing that she has to bring Zipporah back. But for now, she wants to put that woman out of her mind and focus on her man. Cher can feel his manhood stiffening for her. She leans into him and kisses his lips.

"Is all that for me?" she whispers, unbuttoning his shirt.

"And only you, goddess," he says, lifting her dashiki over her head. Cher's bare breasts and eager nipples greet him. He presses his face between them, kissing her breastbone. Cher sighs heavily, running her fingers through his thick, wavy hair. He rubs his hand up the middle of her back and into her hair. He pulls her face to his and kisses her long and hard, sucking on her tongue.

Cher is excited and exhilarated. She wants so badly to feel his love inside of her. Pharaoh can't wait either. His heart races as he watches her step out of her underwear. She helps him remove his sling and his clothes. Cher is used to Pharaoh being on top. He prefers to be in the dominate position, but tonight he gives the sexual authority over to the goddess. Pharaoh sit back down into his chair and beckons for her to come. Cher climbs on his lap. She guides his love inside of her and slides down onto the thickness of his manhood. She feels the sheer ecstasy of him deep inside of her. She has finally adapted to him. The pain is gone and only the pleasure remains.

Pharaoh is ready to burst inside for her when she starts to ride him. The feeling of her love is so overwhelmingly glorious.

"Oh, goddess," he moans loudly. He can't help but express his elation. It has been five days since he experienced her body. He didn't know how badly he needed to have her, how desperately he needed the release until now.

"Ahhh, goddess," Pharaoh shrieks, digging his nails into her hips. His body tenses and his toes curl from the bliss of her love. Cher's head arches back as she rides. Her hair brushes against his thighs, enticing him all the more. Pharaoh's manhood feels so good to her. She can tell that he is backed up. His love is as hard as a sledgehammer. Cher is raptured by the deliciousness of knowing that he has been saving himself for her. They have spent the days apart, but his mind, his heart and his body have remained faithful to her. The ecstasy of her love ravishes him, as she rolls her hips forward. Pharaoh can't hold it back any longer, neither does he want to. He explodes inside of her like a cannon. Pharaoh's orgasm comes in spasmodic waves. Cher rocks on top of him until she is sure that she has received all he has to offer.

Pharaoh rests his sweaty forehead on Cher's chest. She knows Pharaoh well enough now to know that he is not yet completely satisfied, but at least the pressure is off. She can tell, listening to his breaths, that he is relaxed. Pharaoh scoots to the edge of the chair. Cher wraps her legs and arms tightly around him as he stands. He is glad that she is strong enough to support her own weight, so that he doesn't have to strain his shoulder. He lies down on top of her in the bed. He kisses her lips, then lays his head on her collarbone.

"I've been thinking," Pharaoh whispers into her ear. "With Big Mama gone, all Pharaoh has in the world now is Cher."

"Well, who or what else could Pharaoh need but Cher," she says playfully.

"I will tell you what your god desires." He brushes his fingertips along her shoulder. "I have put my life, my seed inside of you and I want you to bring forth children for me."
Cher looks into his eyes. She cannot believe his request.

"Give me a little girl who looks like you and a son who looks just exactly like you. This is what I want goddess; to worship you in three persons. I want to surround myself with your image." Pharaoh kisses her deeply. "Will the goddess give this offering to her god and King?"

"Yes," Cher breathes. "Yes. Quoi que tu souhaites."

Pharaoh smiles as brightly as the sun and her smile like the moon reflects the glory of its rays. Cher places her hands on Pharaoh's cheeks. She didn't know he could make her any happier, until he just did.

"I have a gift for the mother of my heir." Pharaoh reaches over the edge of the bed for his pants. His hand fishes around, then brings up a long slender box. He places the box on the bed and opens it. He holds up a beautiful silver necklace, full of large, twinkling emerald stones for Cher to see, then lays it on her collarbone.

"Thank you, Papa." Cher says enthusiastically. She has finally learned how to accept his gifts graciously. She gets them so often. She kisses him and his passion is reignited.

Pharaoh makes quick work of his request and presses his love inside of her again. He begins to make slow, passionate love to her. Cher can tell that each long, meaningful stroke has a special purpose for him now. Like a farmer, plowing the field he plans to sow, Pharaoh is preparing Cher's body to produce life for him. He fertilizes her with his seed to overflowing yet once more, before falling asleep between her thighs.

# WOMAN TO WOMAN

The next day went by smoother than anyone expected. Pharaoh's lieutenants were concerned about having Big Mama's funeral and memorial services in Long Beach, but Pharaoh insisted that she be buried there between her son, Kingston and her husband, Albert. Pharaoh felt that the Brothers would have more respect for Big Mama than to cause a scene with them on her day.

Furthermore, Pharaoh felt it would be good for the neighborhood to know that Golden Sphinx wasn't gone. Pharaoh and all fifteen of his men went to the funeral for Big Mama. It was a huge event. Big Mama was a mother of the church and a pillar in the community, so a massive congregation of people came to say their farewells. Pharaoh surprised Cher by requesting that instead of dressing in black, everyone in his organization wear white for his grandmother, signifying that she still lives on even though she left this earth.

They showed up at the burial site, looking like an angelic host. Pharaoh brought a giant bouquet of dark red roses and placed them on her coffin. He hid his moist eyes behind large, dark sunglasses, as he sat on the front row beside Cher. She wrapped her hand tightly around his bicep, letting him know that he had her support. After Pharaoh threw a handful of dirt into his grandmother's grave, he and his associates left.

They all assembled at Big Mama's house, following the burial services. Pharaoh had a huge spread of delicious food prepared for the community to come and pay their last respects to Big Mama. It turned into a somewhat festive event with music and dancing in the front yard. Pharaoh was glad. He knew that Big Mama would be proud to see them honoring her with joy instead of mourning.

Cher rolls her eyes and sucks her teeth when Zipporah walks into the house with her tall, fair-skinned boy. Cher is surprised that her son is so old, maybe thirteen, give or take a year. Zipporah's son is almost her mirror image, except for his dark, intense eyes, thick wavy hair and the tiny mole on his right cheek. They look more like salt and pepper siblings than mother and child.

Cher eyes her as she hugs some of the attendants. Cher isn't sure if she buys Pharaoh's story that they never crossed the line. Still, she doesn't want to seem mistrustful of her man, so she approaches Zipporah and asks for a private word with her in Big Mama's bedroom.

"Look, I thought about everything and I've decided to keep you on as my *maid*." Cher says the words with condescendence. "If you still want your job back."

"That's fine. I would be happy to come back... if you'll have me," Zipporah answers meekly with a gentle, courteous smile.

"Just understand that Pharaoh is **mine** and I don't want you to ever get that twisted up in your head. We are solid, so I don't need you up in my house trying to run interference. Do you hear me?" Cher points her finger in Zipporah's face.

"Loud and clear," she says, squaring her shoulders. "Believe me when I say that I am the least of your problems. I am not the one you need to be worried about, honey. You just go right on and enjoy yourself some Pharaoh, while you can. I will stay far out of your way."

Zipporah leaves the room quickly. Cher slides over a few of the coats on the bed, clearing a spot for herself on the edge. Something still didn't feel right in Cher's heart. She didn't expect Zipporah to respond that way. She was hoping that Zipporah would buck on her and give up some information, but what she said didn't make sense to Cher. Something in her tone, or maybe just being in this house, took her back to Big Mama's warning.

Cher didn't know what the appropriate response was.

*Should she be afraid?*

*Should she just leave Pharaoh?*

Cher is so completely caught up with Pharaoh that she can't imagine her life without him now. She loves him. Sure, he is a little possessive and territorial, but all and all, Cher has seen so much good in him. What cause would she have to leave him now?

Cher saw his rage, his unabridged wrath that night on the back street, but he was defending himself and protecting her. Pharaoh had cause to be so relentlessly brutal, their lives were threatened. Cher shook her head, scattering loose all of the negative thoughts. Zipporah was just trying to get inside of her head. Maybe she was hoping to get Cher to forfeit, but Zipporah had another thing coming if she thought she could get Pharaoh by default.

Pharaoh and Cher left around 5pm, before the memorial wrapped up. He took her back to the house. He and his associates had a business meeting to attend. He delegated the task of staying with Cher out to Musah. Since he was resigning from Golden Sphinx Financial, Pharaoh didn't feel he needed to be in attendance. As it stood, Musah needed to rest up for his move the next day. Pharaoh had confidence that even in his debilitated condition, he could still wield some steel and protect Cher if the need arose. So, with much hesitation, it was decided. Pharaoh kissed Cher's cheek and disappeared with his men. He changed the security code before he left, so that no one could get in or out.

Musah spent the evening sitting on the sofa in the living room, watching Pharaoh's big screen rear projection television. Cher never watches it; seems like a screen that big just makes her dizzy. Cher asks Musah if he needs anything; but as usual, Musah doesn't respond to her. He didn't even take his eyes off the screen to acknowledge her. Cher makes a sandwich for herself and one for Musah. She slices his in halves, then puts it on a plate and leaves it on the counter. She wraps hers in a napkin and goes upstairs.

# BOSS NIGGER

"Well Pharaoh, we on day six of our terror campaign against the Italians and it seems to be going pretty good."

Blaze begins the proceedings. "We got six down and only four more to go. Action and Rufus are going to move in on Piscittelli's nephew tonight at his eighteenth birthday party. We got a location for the set up a little over six hundred yards away from the restaurant in an abandoned warehouse."

"Rufus, are you sure you can make that shot?" Pharaoh asks skeptically.

"Blindfolded and hanging upside down with one arm tied behind my back, Pharaoh." He shoots a thumbs-up.

"Action," Pharaoh says, pointing to him. "What's the word with the Italians?"

"They all terrified and shit," Action begins, taking his toothpick from his mouth. "They say they don't know what's going on. They still swearing their innocence and begging for a meeting with you. They say they willing to renegotiate. Whatever terms we want, if we just stop the killings."

"Well..." Pharaoh starts with a smile. "There are people in hell who want ice water, but they're not going to get it. Sit on the Italians until we're done, then set up the meeting and let me know when and where it goes down."

"Roger that." Action replaces his toothpick.

"Jinx, what's the status on the Brothers?" Pharaoh asks, stroking his chin.

"You'd better go to Johnny or Donovan on that one. I've been too busy murdering Italians to keep up with the Brothers. I put them on that detail."

"Okay," Pharaoh replies slowing, eyeing Jinx with irritation. Pharaoh is the only one who is able to delegate responsibility. If he doesn't know who is covering which territory at any given time, it allows for a weak link in the chain of command. Jinx knows better than to override Pharaoh's directives without telling him. However, Pharaoh decides to leave the chastisement for a later time.

"Donovan, give it to me straight." Pharaoh cuts his eyes over to him. Pharaoh is preparing him for promotion to lieutenant after Musah's departure.

"Alright," he replies, licking his thick, dark lips. "I've been beating the drag pretty heavy in Long Beach. It's chaos down there. I had to cap a Brother who tried to shake me down a couple nights ago."

Donovan, who is ordinarily devoid of emotion, seems dismayed by having to give this report. "There are two opposing factions warring it out, the Hoodlum Disciples and the Black Gangster Mafia. Even *if* one could defeat the other, both groups are too disorganized and unstable to have any longevity. It's a murder/ suicide mission for both camps, 'cause all I've seen is a lot of senseless killing and no one appears to be winning. Niggahs jumping ship every day to keep from getting put in a body bag and the ones that ain't getting killed are getting popped by the pigs. All the violence is getting the cops attention, so it won't be long before they raid the ghetto and take whoever's left standing. The second situation is the hustlers who got forced out of the game by the competition. That's the majority of the Brothers that Golden Sphinx was dealing with. They out of business without you and they can't afford the Italians half-ass product, because they had to raise the rates on the Brothers since you pulled out on them too. There was a little bit of talk about an alliance forming between the Brothers and the Italians, but all the negotiations broke down when the Brothers found out that the Italians were the ones who set them up against you. The Brothers are begging for a meeting with you too. They say they need Golden Sphinx to come back and regulate Long Beach."

Johnny joins in the discussion. "All I know, at this point, is that the game is a big, bloody mess right now and I think it's best if we stay as far out of it as possible." Johnny runs his hands over his head. "We've seen shit in Long Beach we didn't think was going to happen. It's falling apart down there. I don't know if we can even salvage what's left and rebuild that branch of the operation."

"That is very disturbing news," Pharaoh says, wrinkling his brow. He sits at the head of the conference table in his large, brown leather chair.

It is after hours and they are in their office building on Ventura Boulevard. From the outside it looks just like any other financial firm in the area, except for the fact that only fly, well-dressed Black men work there on a daily basis. Pharaoh spends the majority of his time at the office, more so than the others, because he is over all the legitimate divisions of operation. Pharaoh, the most articulate and well-spoken of them all, handles the White clientele and does a superior job of swindling them out of whatever money possible with his business savvy.

"This is a very sad state of affairs for Golden Sphinx. I must be honest with you gentlemen. These are not only different times, but drastic ones and they call for drastic measures. The company that cannot adapt is the company that goes under when the seasons change and this, gentlemen,... is the winter of our discontent."

Pharaoh makes a triangle with his fingers and puckers his lips. He is trying to find the words to communicate the gravity of their situation, without causing a panic.

"I have been doing the numbers and for the first time in the history of Golden Sphinx, we are in the red. Deep in the red."

"What?" A collective gasp.

The men look around at each other with astonishment on their faces.

"How can this be happening? I thought you said we were solvent," Mayhem raises his voice.

"Launching this campaign against both Long Beach and the Italians at the same time has cut out two of the highest yielding revenue streams that Golden Sphinx has. I thought we could withstand the hit since the campaign would only last two weeks-tops, but I underestimated the collateral damage that even a couple weeks would cause. I tried redirecting funds into the Financial Firm but the returns have been slower than I expected. In addition, if you haven't heard, Musah is resigning from Golden Sphinx and his shares are going with him."

The conference room breaks out into an uproar. The men stand up out of their seats. Blaze, who is standing against the back wall, and the other lieutenants remain calm. They know Pharaoh better than the others, and therefore do not join in the fuss and commotion. Donovan likewise remains cool, with his eyes focused on Pharaoh.

"I thought you said, 'no one gets in and no one gets out'. What happened to that Pharaoh?" Chaos pounds his fist on the table.

"Whoa, little brother! You need to pump your brakes," Action interrupts. "You don't know Musah like we do. He gave his blood, sweat and tears for this organization."

"And now he just gets to walk out when we need him?" Deitricks asks maliciously. "Since Golden Sphinx is going under, what if I say I want out too?"

Pharaoh is instantly enraged. He senses mutiny on his ship and he will not tolerate it. Pharaoh walks over to Deitricks and presses his palm seemingly effortlessly into the center of his chest.

Deitricks hits the ground hard, sucking desperately for air and slides into the back wall. Pharaoh's blow knocked all of the wind out him, leaving only a tight, stinging sensation that cannot be satisfied by his quick, labored gasps.

Pharaoh has never struck one of his men and all of the lieutenants look concerned when they witness it. They know that there's something Pharaoh is not telling anyone, because they have never seen him this upset before.

"This is the house that Pharaoh's hands built and I'll be damned before I let you tear it down. You will respect me," Pharaoh says with fragile control.

His body trembles, as he speaks. "It was my name and my reputation that built this company. Don't you **ever** forget that. My skills and my cunning... My plan made this operation a success. Back when I was in Nam, I didn't spend my money on opium or Vietnamese whores or impressive rides. I made sacrifices and brought all the cash I could save back to the U.S. I turned that first $10,000 into $100,000 on the back of my own ghetto hustle, then flipped it into a legitimate company and brought in the first million Golden Sphinx ever made **by myself**– by my fucking self, Deitricks." Pharaoh stands over him, yelling seemingly only at him, but Pharaoh is making this exhibition for everyone in the room to understand and never question his authority again.

"I came back for each and every one of my men. I took you from your minimum wage construction jobs, your mama's houses, and the homeless shelter. I even went and got you out of the pen, Deitricks," Pharaoh huffs sardonically.

"I trained each of you in the hustle. I fed you knowledge and wisdom from my very own hand like babies. I took you from the bottom rung on the ladder in a country that didn't give a fuck about you– a country that gave you its ass to kiss. I gave each of you an office in my New World Order. I shared a huge slice of

American pie with you and this is how you repay me."

Deitricks begins to turn blue. He still isn't able to fully inflate his lungs. He can only sip enough air to make it to the next second. The pain and pressure on his chest is so intense that he blinks involuntary tears. Deitricks feels like a fish out of water and every second until he gasps again feels like his last.

"I made Golden Sphinx viable. I made this organization into something we could be proud of, something more than a criminal band of gangsters. It is under my authority and because of my leadership that we all live in luxury, comfort and safety." Pharaoh pounds his fist against his chest.

He glances up from Deitricks, who is finally regaining his color as he collects a slowly increasing amount of oxygen. Pharaoh's eyes scan the faces in the room. The lieutenants are nodding their agreement with Pharaoh and confirming their unwavering allegiance to him.

Pharaoh's tone flips from fierce to lighthearted and whimsical. "Has anyone in this room ever gone a day without what they needed because of Golden Sphinx?" Pharaoh lifts his hand in the air. "Just raise your hand if you have," he says playfully.

Everyone remains motionless in the conference room, eyes locked on Pharaoh while he paces in a short revolution.

"Anybody here... ever did a day of jail time because of Golden Sphinx?"

No hands go up.

"*Nobody?*" Pharaoh asks facetiously, with a pout on his face. "How about this one?" He taps his finger against his bottom lip. "Anybody in this room ever take a bullet for Golden Sphinx?"

Pharaoh's is the lone hand that raises in the room. He turns around so that everyone can see that his hand is up.

"The only other man that I know of to be in this company with me is Musah. He's the only man in this organization that laid his life on the line for it. He almost died in my basement and excuse me if I think that is sacrifice enough. He wanted to stay on with us. He would not have left, but I released him. I can't ask any more of him than what he has given."

Benny's eyes are sad, as he listens to Pharaoh's words. He knows that Pharaoh is doing right by Musah.

Pharaoh continues on, "I would do the same for any one of you in his position. Musah risked his life and that is what brought him his release from this organization. So Deitricks, to answer your question, if you are ready to offer your resignation—" Pharaoh snaps his fingers towards Jinx who tosses him his Browning. Pharaoh aims it right at the middle of Deitricks chest. "I'd be more than happy to help arrange that for you," Pharaoh states cordially.

Deitricks realizes that he has been very disrespectful, but he knows that groveling in front of Pharaoh will get him killed faster than his rebellion. He gets up from the ground; rising slowly since he is still lightheaded. His chest continues to sting but he can finally breathe well enough to talk.

"I apologize, Pharaoh. I lost my head for a moment." Deitricks humbles himself, dropping his eyes in front of him. "I was out of line, but my question was only hypothetical. I needed guidance and I thank you for offering it to me." His words are sincere. Deitricks knows that he was wrong to pull rank on Pharaoh like that. Pharaoh has been too good to Deitricks for him to behave that way.

"Okay," Pharaoh says, lowering the gun. He hugs him tightly around the shoulders. "Pharaoh will forgive this time." Pharaoh tosses the Browning back to Jinx and returns to his seat at the head of the table.

"If no one has any other objections, then I would like to propose my plan. Since we may not be able to reopen the Long Beach operation, I believe it is time to add two new bodies and expand to Vegas. We have talked about it before and I think it is the only hope for the future of Golden Sphinx."

Everyone looks around nervously. They are not sure if the proposal is up for discussion in light of Pharaoh's present mood.

"All in favor?" he asks, making it clear that he is not welcoming any further debate on the matter.

Seven hands go up. All of the lieutenants, Donovan and Jeepers still represent only half of the organization's members. Ordinarily, Pharaoh does not vote on these matters; including Musah, there are fifteen members under his command. There has never been a tie before, so Pharaoh exercises his executive power and casts the deciding vote.

"Blaze, you are the spearhead for the Vegas expansion." Pharaoh immediately dictates his orders. Blaze gives him an informal, two-finger salute. "Pick one of our own and present your submissions for the two new recruits to your team tomorrow. We will begin to coordinate the plans for the Vegas operation then. In the meantime, everyone else stay put... Rufus–" Pharaoh calls him out.

"I'll be checking the paper in the morning to see if you made that shot. This meeting is now adjourned."

# IF THERE'S A HELL BELOW

Pharaoh returns to the house late, a little after 1 am. He stayed behind at the office and crunched numbers for hours. He wanted to be able to give Blaze the specifics for the estimated expenses and returns on the Vegas expansion project. Pharaoh had to plug different monetary amounts into his formulas to see what the projected yield would be for each investment. After he was satisfied that he had enough thorough research to present to the organization, he locked up the office and went home.

Cher is asleep when he tiptoes into their bedroom. Boredom took its toll on her hours earlier and she has been asleep for quite some time. Pharaoh decides to forgo his night shower, not wanting to wake Cher. He strips out of all his clothes and steps into a pair of navy lounge pants. Pharaoh slips down into the bed with her, wrapping his arm around her waist, and falls asleep.

****

Cher wakes up abruptly. She is choking. Pharaoh straddles her chest, with his large hands wrapped around her throat. He is strangling her mercilessly. Cher gasps for air but his grip tightens every time she breathes out. Between his weight on her chest and his hands around her neck, Cher is sure she's a goner. Her ears pop from the pressure in her head and she can feel her chest bone shift. Pharaoh's eyes are completely black again. She can tell that he is absent. She wants to call his name, but she can't even remember what it is, as she begins to lose consciousness.

Cher's mind scrambles with its last ounce of lucidity. She reaches out for the bedside table. Her hand grasps frantically until her fingers close around a glass vase. With her last ounce of strength, she smashes it against the side of Pharaoh's head.

His hands release her and he reaches for his face. Blood spills from the wound and rolls down the side of his cheek. Cher catches her breath and begins to scream. More because she is afraid that she has hurt Pharaoh than anything else.

"Baby are you okay?" she wails. Pharaoh falls to the floor, clutching the gash. Cher parts his fingers trying to see how badly he is cut.

"Is everything alright up there?" Musah's voice comes across the intercom.

Cher is too busy, pressing a cloth to Pharaoh's head to answer. Pharaoh regains his bearings and staggers to his feet. He shakes his head, feeling his senses coming back to him.

"What's going on, Cher?" He stares at her blankly. Pharaoh takes the cloth from her and wipes the side of his face. He looks at his own blood with disbelief; and then looks back at Cher with an inaudible *why* in his eyes.

"I'm coming up," Musah declares over the intercom.

Before he can reach the second level, Pharaoh meets him on the top stair. There is concern in Musah's expression when he sees the blood on Pharaoh's face and hands. Musah stands panting and pressing his hand over the bandage on his own chest.

"Are you alright, Musah?" Pharaoh asks with just as much concern in his tone.

"Sure, Boss. I'm fine. I should be asking you that question." Musah points to his face.

"Oh, I'm cool," Pharaoh replies dismissively. "I just fell out of bed. I must have hit something on the way down– maybe the edge of the nightstand."

Musah sighs his relief. "It sounded like you were killing yourself up there."

Pharaoh laughs lightly at Musah's expense. "Let me go get this wound cleaned up and you get the rest of your nap out, my friend. You have a very long trip ahead of you tomorrow."

"You sure everything's alright, Boss?"

"Yeah. Cher is going to take care of me," he answers

assuredly, patting Musah on the shoulder.

"Okay." Musah hesitates, then begins his trek back down the stairs.

When Pharaoh returns to the room, Cher is still trembling on the edge of the bed.

"I am so sorry Cher," Pharaoh whispers sincerely, as he sits down beside her. He tilts her head to the side and examines the large, purple fingerprints on her neck. She has extensive bruising all around her throat and some on her chest too. "Did I do this to you?"

Cher is surprised that he doesn't remember what happened. She watches him suspiciously, not sure if his obliviousness is genuine. His face is tender and he is as wide-eyed as a young child.

"What the hell did I do?" He asks seemingly to himself, as he lightly brushes her neck with his fingers. "I swear I didn't mean it. I have these night rages sometimes because of my years in Nam. I haven't shared my bed with anyone in years. I didn't know I still had them." He buries his head in disappointment. "I can sleep in the bedroom on the west wing from now on if you want me to." He looks up at her from under his hands with sad, remorseful eyes.

"No, Papa. I'm fine. I just wish I knew about this before now."

"I apologize, goddess. I would have told you if I thought it was something you had to worry about. It doesn't really happen that often, but I have never hurt anyone when I had them. Usually I just ball up in a corner, or wake up trembling in a puddle of my own urine." Pharaoh drops his eyes. "It's actually quite embarrassing and it's something that I don't like to share with anyone. That's why I rarely sleep with you, but sometimes I just need to feel you in my arms. It's the only thing that can put me to sleep some nights; but I will stay away, if it means keeping you safe."

Cher's heart is full of compassion for him. Her little god-king can be so delicate and fragile. She wraps her arms around his shoulders.

"I love you, my King." She reassures her man. "It is fine. We will be alright." She smiles, then says jokingly. "The goddess will forgive this time."

Pharaoh returns her smile and pecks tiny, eager kisses on her lips. They clean each other up. Cher uses peroxide to disinfect Pharaoh's wound, which turns out to be little more than a long scratch on his scalp. Pharaoh applies a warm compress to Cher's neck and gives her a light shoulder massage with myrrh oil, to relax her and expedite the healing process.

They slept in late the next morning. They needed the rest and the recuperation from an eventful night. They lay in the bed together, kissing and petting each other; trying to mend their relationship more than their bodies.

Musah is completely packed and Benny calls on the intercom to be let in the front gate, before Pharaoh finally rises from the bed. He and Cher pull on their long decorative Caftans. Cher pulls her puffy hair forward, trying to cover the bruises on her neck and chest. She doesn't want anyone to think more of it than it is. Once she is satisfied with her appearance, she drifts downstairs with Pharaoh.

Musah and Pharaoh say their goodbyes at the front door, hugging each other as tightly as blood brothers. Benny helps Musah carry his few suitcases to the car. Cher and Pharaoh stand at the door while the men pack the trunk. Cher looks over and sees that Musah's rucksack is still sitting on the floor of the foyer. She grabs it and hops quickly down the front steps.

"Here you go, Musah," she says enthusiastically. Musah doesn't even look at her. Cher wanted to believe that since he was leaving he would be more cordial. She just tosses his backpack in the trunk and turns to go back up the steps.

"I think you may need help," Musah breathes lowly, with his eyes still focused in the trunk. Cher turns to him, but she still isn't sure he is talking to her. Musah moves his lips and stares off in the distance, as if he is rehearsing and choosing the right words.

"I think you're in trouble," he states quietly. Cher walks back up to Musah. She figures he is doing this so that Pharaoh won't know that he is talking to her. Cher tries not to give it away in her face and looks at Benny who is placing a bag in the back seat. Musah sighs in defeat, dropping his eyes again. "You just take care of yourself alright. Please, don't let that demon control you." He whispers the words like a prayer and slams the trunk closed.

When Cher glances up at Pharaoh, his eyes are angry and she can tell that he is incensed. She trots back up the steps to his side. Musah and Benny wave before getting into the car. Pharaoh and Cher see them off as they pull away down the drive.

Zipporah returned to the house that afternoon and things were noticeably different. She paid Cher absolutely no attention, like she wasn't even there. Zipporah only marginally regarded Pharaoh enough to accomplish his requests. Zipporah just zipped around the house, tidying up, dusting tables, folding laundry and then after she prepared dinner for them, she left. Cher was glad that their talk had set things straight.

Pharaoh and Cher had a candlelit dinner alone together in their big empty house. Cher was glad, after such a busy week, to finally have Pharaoh all to herself. Likewise, Pharaoh was happy to be back in his home and not be lonely anymore.

"Who is Belle?" Cher asks innocently, lifting a forkful of

green beans into her mouth.

A look of sudden terror comes over Pharaoh's face, like he has just seen a ghost. Pharaoh does his best to hide his expression from Cher, chewing quickly and wiping his mouth with a cloth napkin.

"Why do you ask?" Pharaoh raises his brow.

"Well..." Cher begins hesitantly. "Last night you were calling me Belle while you were choking me."

"I do apologize again, goddess." He surrenders his palms to her. "I am sending you to the spa in the morning. I really feel terrible about that."

"And I have forgiven you," she replies mildly. "So... who is Belle?"

"I don't know any Belle," Pharaoh blurts nervously.

Cher has never seen this side of him. Usually Pharaoh is so forthcoming. It is strange for him to try to hide something from her.

"Pharaoh, you have asked for honesty from me and I have given it." Cher's eyes sharpen, as she watches him from across the long table. "The goddess requires the same."

Pharaoh found her tone strange. She was more forward and direct than he was used to. He felt the balance of authority tip in her favor and he didn't like it. Still, his word was the law and even he was subject to it.

"Okay, goddess." He sits back in his tall, golden chair. "Belle was my wife at one time, many years ago."

"You never told me that you were married."

"You never asked," Pharaoh retorts shortly.
Cher is visibly dismayed by the revelation.

"There are many things that I have not told you, but that doesn't mean I hid anything from you. There are also many things that you have not told me, but it will all come out in time."

Cher doesn't let Pharaoh's eloquence get him off the hook.

She continues the pursuit.

"What happened between you and Belle?"

Pharaoh can see that Cher will not be deterred, so he cracks the door for her to peek inside the tomb of his past.

"We were young when we got married shortly after I came back from Nam. We lived together for about four years and then she left me." Pharaoh offers the short narrative and then resigns, hoping that has satisfied Cher's curiosity.

But it wasn't sufficient, so Cher asks, "Why did she leave you?" trying to find the answers to the questions that Zipporah and Musah have raised in her heart.

Pharaoh sighs and then answers, "If you ever find her, then maybe you can ask her that question yourself; because she is the only one who knows. She ran off with one of my men... a lieutenant named Jimmy. Last I heard, they are happy together somewhere near Reno."

"If you know where she is why don't you try to get her back?" Cher pushes the subject.

Pharaoh's frustration shows. He takes his napkin from his lap and throws it on his plate.

"I told you that Pharaoh does not want what is not his. She made her choice and I made mine. Belle is dead to me." Pharaoh stands and leaves the table.

Cher is instantly upset with herself for pressing Pharaoh and making him angry. She is beginning to see how sensitive he is about his past. Cher decides to give him some time to cool off while she clears the table and cleans the dishes. Cher is surprised when she comes into the bedroom to find Pharaoh waiting naked on the bed for her. He made passionate love to her for hours before he let her rest. They slept soundly that night, but this time it was not Pharaoh- but Cher who had the nightmare.

\*\*\*\*

*Cher never thought that seeing her mother again would be a nightmare... but it is. Her mother is dressed all in black and she has a large, gaping slash in her throat. The jagged skin that hangs from her neck flaps open when she moves and blood spills from the tear all over her long, wavy hair.*

*"Cher," she says frantically, reaching for her arm. Her mother is removing large stacks of money from a safe. "Get the money!" she exclaims, extending the bills towards her. Cher is dressed completely in black as well and has a large, brown-leather satchel. Her mother tosses what seems like thousands and thousands of dollars into the bag, still bleeding profusely the entire time. The bills are slick with blood.*

*"Why Mama?" Cher calls with a frightened voice. "Why?"*

*Cher is asking her mother why she left her that day thirteen years ago and why she didn't just stay there in the trailer with her until the police came.*

*"Hide, ma petite!" she yells, pushing Cher's shoulder. "Just hide, Cher."*

Cher scares awake. She lays panting and sweating in the moonlight. Pharaoh is still asleep with his arm laying across her stomach. She calms herself quickly. She doesn't want to wake him. She needs the quiet time away from him to sort this whole thing out. Cher couldn't ignore the warnings anymore and she couldn't ignore the dreams. Someone or something was trying to get a message to Cher and it was time she finally listened.

*Pharaoh Forever*

# TO BE CONTINUED...

*Pharaoh Forever*

*Devian Nikei*

# About the Author

Devian Nikei is a native of Charlotte, North Carolina. This actress, singer/songwriter, host. choreographer and entertainer is also an author and publisher. She is the owner of Nikei Novels Publishing and the creator of her parent company and trademark brand Deviance By Devian. Her companies offer a myriad of products including, books and fragrances as well as services such as vocal and life coaching. She is currently working on new music, novels and stage plays. Friends and followers can connect with her latest releases and events by subscribing to her website: www.deviancebydevian.com.

Also, be sure to read other titles by this author